not like us

(an ilse beck fbi suspense thriller—book 1)

ava strong

Ava Strong

Debut author Ava Strong is author of the REMI LAURENT mystery series, comprising three books (and counting); of the ILSE BECK mystery series, comprising four books (and counting); and o the STELLA FALL psychological suspense thriller series, comprising three books (and counting).

An avid reader and lifelong fan of the mystery and thriller genres Ava loves to hear from you, so please feel free to visit www.avastrongauthor.com to learn more and stay in touch._

ISBN: 978-1-0943-9214-1

BOOKS BY AVA STRONG

REMI LAURENT FBI SUSPENSE THRILLER
THE DEATH CODE (Book #1)
THE MURDER CODE (Book #2)
THE MALICE CODE (Book #3)

ILSE BECK FBI SUSPENSE THRILLER
NOT LIKE US (Book #1)
NOT LIKE HE SEEMED (Book #2)
NOT LIKE YESTERDAY (Book #3)
NOT LIKE THIS (Book #4)

STELLA FALL PSYCHOLOGICAL SUSPENSE THRILLER
HIS OTHER WIFE (Book #1)
HIS OTHER LIE (Book #2)
HIS OTHER SECRET (Book #3)

CHAPTER ONE

Her thumb wavered above the tarmac, the tips of her sneakers brushing the white line painted on the edge of the meandering highway. Sarah Beth frowned beneath the night as another car swished by, kicking up dust and prompting a crackling flurry of leaves against the concrete barrier behind her.

She muttered darkly, keeping her hand up in the night, but raising a different finger now in the direction of the speeding sedan.

Once the car was out of sight, she lowered her hand, shivering where she stood on the side of the road just outside Seattle. The surroundings of the city were normally bathed in mist, even during the day, but now, under the cover of darkness and cloud, the only illumination came from the highway lights spread at fifty-foot intervals, and the occasional headlights of passing vehicles, though those were rare enough too.

Sarah Beth shifted one shoulder, feeling a crick in her neck and wincing, rubbing at her upper arm and lowering her backpack to the ground.

Fifteen cars now… Fifteen cars had ignored her.

She sighed. The average was twenty-two. She'd taken to counting ever since she'd fled the group home four years ago. They'd said she'd get herself hurt, trying to live on her own. They'd said she wouldn't make it a week.

Well, now, four years later, having turned twenty-one last month, she'd proven them all wrong. A life on the move, on the road, in box cars, or beneath underpasses, using gym showers or working for room and board wasn't most people's version of the American Dream. But Sarah Beth was free. More free than anyone she knew. A few uncomfortable nights, sleeping in a Walmart parking lot or tidying up in a Planet Fitness bathroom, was a small price to pay for freedom.

When it came to such things, though, it was always a bit of a balancing act. How much makeup to wear? How clean to look? On one hand, if she was too groomed and prettied up, often the entirely wrong sorts would stop to give her a ride. Though she had a gut feeling for these types of men.

On the other hand, if she abandoned grooming standards entirely, then no one would want her in their car.

Sarah Beth reached up and brushed her curly brown hair back behind her ears, while practicing her smile. She'd been told more than once that she had a very pretty smile.

She glanced back down the highway, her shoulder still aching, a soft chill falling over her. She shuffled a bit on the side of the road, her left leg prompting a wince as she readjusted her weight and half-limped into a more comfortable standing position.

She saw the truck before she heard it.

First, bright headlights, too far off the ground to come from a sedan. A second later, as the truck dipped over the road, the lights lowering, she spotted the large blue cab and the flatbed behind it.

Hastily, she brushed her hair back again, this time risking a full-toothed smile—like someone in the theater overacting for the sake of the audience in the back of the room—and jutted her thumb up. She leaned in just a bit, toeing the white line now and staring into the glare of the approaching headlights.

Her stomach twisted and her smile began to flicker as the truck showed no signs of slowing down. On it came, faster, faster…

Then, a screech of brakes.

The lights dimmed and the large vehicle came to a jarring stop only a few paces ahead of Sarah Beth. She swallowed, staring at where the vehicle had gone still.

A hand waved through the open window, gesturing at her. No sound, no words, just a single flick of the wrist.

Sarah Beth leaned forward, peering up at the face in the cab. "You going to Seattle?" she called out.

Again, no audible response. Just a quick flash of a thumbs-up and another gesture of a beckoning hand, like a flapping bird beneath the glow of the moon.

Sarah Beth hesitated, staring up at the truck and swallowing. A second later, the flapping hand disappeared back into the truck and then a single yellow Post-it note fluttered to the ground, tossed from the window.

Sarah Beth frowned even deeper now. She leaned down hesitantly, eyes firmly on the truck, but fingers scrambling for the note.

She hadn't heard any scribbling, and in fact, the letters on the note were written in pen, as if perhaps the note had been written before. Was the driver mute?

Sarah Beth held up the note and read, simply: *Hop in!* followed by a little smiley face. Sarah Beth looked up uneasily, holding the note between her fingertips which now made a crinkling sound similar to the leaves against the concrete barrier. The cold was oppressive, and it was only getting darker.

The roads were more abandoned than she'd first imagined.

Besides, the trucker was smiling now, too, flashing a friendly look from inside the driver's side. Not mute, but maybe a bit dumb? Sarah Beth could deal with dumb. In fact, she preferred it. People who thought too much gave her anxiety.

"Thanks," she said, nodding and crumpling the note before placing it back in her pocket. "Honestly, anywhere in the city will do."

She stepped up to the passenger side and slid into the front seat. She kept her backpack at her feet, just in case she needed to beat a hasty retreat.

"I'm Sarah Beth," she said, not expecting a reply now. "Nice to meet you! Thanks much. You really saved me there."

The driver was still smiling beneath a hat with a low brim, shadows across his features. The truck was surprisingly clean, and smelled faintly of air freshener.

For some reason this caused Sarah Beth to relax a bit, her head brushing against the headrest now as the truck churned back to life and began to eat up the gravel road once more. The headlights remained dim as they picked up speed, moving along the highway, heading toward the city.

The driver didn't talk, didn't make moves, didn't try to solicit anything—financial, physical, or otherwise. As far as hitchhiking went, it was starting to look pleasant.

Sarah Beth shot a sidelong glance at her temporary chauffeur. She frowned a second later, noticing a thin trail of scar tissue around the fellow's wrist, just beneath his jacket sleeve.

"You okay, mister?" she asked.

Another thumbs-up. She wondered if perhaps the scar tissue made its way up to the man's neck. Perhaps he couldn't speak at all. She shivered at the thought, feeling a jolt of sympathy as the truck bumped along the old road. She glanced out into the night once more, watching the passing trees. Every so often, she'd surreptitiously use the mirrors to keep an eye on her would-be rescuer.

A girl could never be too careful in the lonely Northwest.

As she considered this, the truck jarred suddenly, taking a turn onto an access road beneath a bright yellow sign.

"Hey, mister," she said, her brow furrowed. "That's not the turn."

The driver didn't reply, sitting like an automaton, glued to the wheel, eyes fixed ahead.

"Mister," Sarah Beth said, louder now. "Please, hey—where are we going?"

Now she had the good sense to feel a sudden jolt of fright shooting through her. The access road gave way to a long-dead farm field. The dust and mud kicked up around them as the tires bumped and jounced, carrying the occupants of the truck quickly away from the highway.

Sarah Beth's heart raced; she edged against the door, distancing herself from the driver. "Mister!" she said. "Where are we going?"

The driver continued ignoring her, and—if anything—now picked up the pace along the old farm road across from the dead field. Beneath the darkening sky, the barren ground and turned dirt against a gray landscape almost seemed like a giant, fresh grave.

"Hey!" Sarah Beth protested now, all attempts at manners fleeing in the face of a surge of fear. "Let me out! I mean it—let me out now!" Her fingers scrambled against the door handle, even though they were still moving.

But it wouldn't open. She yanked at the thing, her fingers grazing cool metal, her knuckles against rough plastic. The door handle moved, but the door remained shut.

"Let me out!" she screamed now. She tried to roll down the window. Also locked.

Suddenly, the truck began to slow with the same jolting, scraping sound as it had on the highway. Dust kicked up in a cloud all around them.

The driver stopped, and Sarah Beth yelled as his hand reached toward her. A hand wearing a thick workman's glove. But it didn't strike her, nor did it seem to hold a weapon. Rather, now, as the dust settled about them outside the old dead field, the driver handed her another sticky note.

She stared, breathing heavily. "I don't know what you're playing at—" she began, her voice shaking.

But the gloved hand just pushed the sticky note toward her more insistently.

Sarah Beth accepted it with trembling fingers if only to have something to do. She glanced down, breathing heavily, though still keeping the driver in her line of sight. Why had he taken her off the road? What were they doing back here? Nothing good—no doubt. Nothing good ever came of things like this. She'd heard stories… horrible stories.

Still, she read the note. And her heart fell into her stomach. Three sentences, though it took her a moment to make them out in the dark. As if sensing her difficulty, the driver reached up and flicked on the cabin light.

Sarah Beth read:

Run. I'll give you a ten-second head start. Then I'm going to slit your throat.

Her heart felt like it went still for a moment. Another little smiley face was drawn on top of the note, like the other one. Again, she hadn't seen the driver write anything, suggesting, perhaps, he'd prepared the notes.

Run.

Her hand still shaking, she looked up and out the front windshield, her eyes as wide as saucers, refusing to glance toward the driver now. No sense encouraging him.

"I—please," she said, blubbering. "*Please.*"

Then she heard the driver's voice for the first time. A low, husky, painful-sounding voice. "One… Two…"

The locks clicked.

"Mister, please!" Sarah Beth pleaded. "Just let me go! I won't tell anyone—honest! Please!"

"Three… Four…"

She cursed, reaching for the handle, grabbing her backpack. The door, to her relief, clicked open. Then, stumbling, gasping, Sarah Beth landed on uneven, muddy ground. She began to sprint, racing off the road, away from the truck.

Then I'll slit your throat.

She shivered. A head start. Whatever sick game this twist was playing, she had a head start. Couldn't stay on the road, though. If she did, the psycho would just run her over. Off the road. Through the trees. Go! Go!

Sarah Beth's heart hammered, pounding wildly.

"Ten!" the voice shouted behind her, clearer, less raspy than before. Almost as if it were excited.

Sarah Beth stumbled through the first row of trees bordering the farmer's field. She tripped over a root but kept going, moving in the dark, trying to navigate undergrowth and low-hanging branches in the sheer black, with no lights to speak of save the faint glow from the truck's headlights behind her.

Then, a clicking sound. The lights turned off.

She heard a thump of the truck's door, followed by the rapid footfalls of pursuit.

Her adrenaline surged wildly. Gasping, sobbing, she ricocheted off a tree with a painful *thump.*

"Please!" she sobbed. "Please!" But there was no one to hear her scream. Her sounds were likely only aiding the driver in tracking her down.

She stumbled through the dark, her shoulder brushing against rough bark, her head glancing off a bending bough. Sharp, jagged branches scraped at her cheeks. Her fingers felt numb where they gripped the strap to her backpack.

She paused for a moment, breathing heavily, trying to plot her path through a nearly invisible undergrowth in the dark.

Behind her, the sound of pursuit had faded.

Sarah Beth exhaled softly, glancing one way then the other… No sign. No light at all. She could barely see her fingers in front of her face.

Which direction had she come from? Where was the truck? Maybe, if she doubled back…

Yes. She might be able to get to the vehicle and run away. At least she'd know the path back to the highway.

Trembling, shaking, adrenaline surging, she began to turn around, moving now in a circling motion through trees, trying her best to step lightly.

For a moment, in the dark, she thought she heard a sound.

Sarah Beth froze, pushing a shoulder against a tree and pressing against it if only for the comforting support of something rigid against her back. Breathing heavily, gasping, she looked around, blinking rapidly, desperately willing her eyes to adjust to the darkness. She glimpsed shadows, outlines of shapes… But not much more.

She wanted to cry for help. But who would hear her? Only the driver.

So she swallowed back her scream, breathing shallowly now, listening… Only listening.

And then a soft whisper of a voice in her ear behind her, against the tree itself. The same raspy, pained voice. "This isn't personal, dear. I did warn you."

Sarah Beth screamed, trying to turn. But a strong hand yanked hard at her hair, jerking her back, her cheek slamming into the rough bark. Then something sharp jabbed against her throat. A sudden flare of pain, an attempt to scream, but no sound would come.

The last thought Sarah Beth had as she crumpled to the ground, bleeding out, was how quietly the driver had moved in the woods. She hadn't even heard him sneak up behind her, like a ghost in the night.

CHAPTER TWO

The wide, pale eyes of a child peered up at the scissors...

"Come here, Hilda," the voice murmured in the dark basement. "Come here *now.*"

The child hyperventilated, shivering and standing in dusty, dirty clothing to match the basement itself. Her eyes traced past the man with the scissors, toward the stairs behind him. Concrete slabs led up to a locked metal door.

Her gaze swished back to her father... back to the single, blunt metal key dangling around his neck.

She swallowed once, hearing the soft whimpering sounds of her siblings behind her, where they lay on their sleeping blankets on the cold concrete.

"Come here, Hilda," the voice repeated, sharply. "I won't repeat it again. I'm only going to cut your hair. I promise."

The child stood stiff, braced like a rabbit ready to bolt. Her father was already breathing heavily, one hand buttressed against the bottom of the stairwell, a thin veneer of sweat across his forehead, his eyes fixed on hers. She could smell the anger, sense it in his every flickering motion. See the rage boiling beneath.

The moment he'd picked up the scissors, she'd run... Run fast, around and around the dusty, dilapidated furniture as he'd tried to catch her. She'd dove beneath the old oak table used for "family meals." She'd run, even knocking over a chair. The moment she'd heard the splintering sound, she'd known she would pay. Still, of all her siblings, she was the one who ran most. Fleeing the inevitable.

"Only my hair?" she whispered, a tinge of hope to her voice.

"Yes, Hilda. Why must you make this so difficult? Come here. Look, see—just a haircut. Don't run again, Hilda, or I'll have to hurt you."

The child stared at her father, wincing. His mismatched eyes glared down at her—one blue, one brown, both full of rage. She knew he was probably lying. He often did. The kinder his tone became, the gentler it was, the more likely the dishonesty.

Then again, what choice did she have? Eventually, if she kept trying to avoid him, her father would call one of her bigger siblings. They'd restrain her, and he'd use the scissors anyway.

She sighed in soft resignation and stepped forward, toward the base of the stairs where her father stood.

He pounced with a victorious cry, his face twisting now into a tapestry of rage. His hand yanked at her small arm, dragging her forward; the scissors flashed down.

Only your hair.

Of course, he'd been lying. He always did...

Ilse Beck's eyes snapped open, fixating on the client who sat across from her on the soft couch. The memories of ten-year-old Hilda Mueller were replaced now by those of thirty-two-year-old Ilse Beck. Ilse stared wide-eyed for a moment at her client—whose eyes were also closed for the memory exercise. Ilse swallowed, clenching her fist slowly, one hand reaching up to probe at her ear... Part of one lobe missing, long since scarred. A wound from more than twenty years ago.

She shivered at the memory, her fingers trailing along her cheek with the healed scar. As the silence stretched, she recited the words in her mind, *Lindholm. Brown hair. Blue eyes. Twenty-eighteen. Four victims. Released. Compulsive behavior...* Slowly, her eyes settled on her client across from her; she forced herself to calm, glancing over her client's shoulder, through the glass patio windows at the gray lake surrounded by large homes and green trees.

For a moment, her gaze on the swishing, chill waters beneath the dark skies, she found her heartbeat steadying. Inhale, exhale, slowly. The scent of the water, the chill air through the mosquito screen wafted over her cheeks. She glanced down at her clothes—a turtleneck sweater and sweatpants. Good enough for work. The clients never seemed to mind. Besides, many of them found the unprofessional, relaxed nature of her lakefront home office and easy demeanor to be calming.

Then her client, eyes still closed, murmured, "I'm sorry, Dr. Beck, but I don't think this is working."

Ilse's attention fixated back on her client, zeroing in. The woman had neat blonde hair tied back in a ponytail, and two heart-shaped earrings framing a pleasant face.

Ilse's own hair was more black than brown. She reached up and brushed at her bangs. Unlike most women, though, instead of pushing her fringe back behind her ear, she brushed it forward, hiding the missing lobe and most of the scar.

"That's quite all right, Samantha," she said, softly. "We can try something else."

The blonde-haired woman opened her eyes. "Just Sam, please."

Ilse held up an apologetic hand. "Sam, great. I know this is only our first session, Sam, but I hope you know I'm here to help."

"I know… I—It's just…" Sam's voice trailed off, an edge to it. Her eyes shifted toward the door. For a moment, it seemed like she might bolt.

"We can go at whatever pace you like," Ilse said, in a soft, soothing voice. "It's your call. It's under your control."

Sam braced in her chair, her fingers white against the armrests, but she seemed to calm a bit. "He's hunting me," she whispered. "I know it. I'm not making it up."

Ilse continued speaking in her soothing tone. "The memory exercise will help us. I promise. Would you like to try again?"

Samantha paused for a moment, biting her lip. Her eyes wide, pupils dilated—terror across every inch of her posture. She gave the faintest, most furtive shake of her head, glancing once more toward the glass door of the patio that led to the hall, and the exit.

Ilse uncrossed her arms, placing them delicately on the armrests of her chair. An open posture, subtle but physical communication. She brushed a thumb past her ear, pushing her hair forward again. She liked wearing her dark hair long and loose. No scrunchies or headbands except when she trained at the gym.

Her features were unmistakably feminine, though she didn't go out of the way to advertise. An upturned, celestial nose and large, searching green eyes made her pretty in a natural, understated sort of way. Ilse had a preference for sweaters and turtlenecks, sweatpants and sandals. She didn't wear makeup, though she was a big fan of cleanliness and grooming. She had no piercings, and only a single tattoo around her wrist. She glanced down at it, rubbing at the long sleeve of her sweater. The tattoo was visible just beneath the cuff, looping her wrist like a handcuff or a manacle. The words of the tattoo read:

Take captive every thought…

Her new client, Sam, leaned back, wincing and crossing her own arms. A defensive, guarded posture. It was only their first session after all. Samantha Wright had been referred to her by a colleague. From what little Ilse had been told, Sam was exactly the sort of case she specialized working with.

But so far, Samantha seemed hesitant to open up.

Ilse considered this a moment, considered the defensive posture of her client—the crossed arms, the tightened lips. The fluttering eyelids even when closed; the askance glances out the window and toward the door. Ilse ran through the likely culprits, the thoughts coming as easily to her as lyrics from an old tune: *Non-integrated emotional trauma. Paranoia? Perhaps. Minimal temperamental and environment protective factors. Psychosomatic anxiety, manifesting in guarded behavior.*

Ilse got slowly to her feet, moving over to the desk placed beneath one of the open windows. She made a big show of opening the window a bit further, and then she sat, resettling in the chair by the desk.

The window was irrelevant, but in this new sitting position, they were now a bit further apart, and instead of sitting directly across from Sam, Ilse was facing the lake as well, shoulder to shoulder. A non-confrontational posture. *Diminishing necessity for protective defenses.* Ilse went quiet, breathing in, out, slowly, waiting, allowing Sam to speak first.

Control. Allowing the client control over the session. Control over her attention. Control over the pace of conversation.

Small methods, but all of them designed to help relax the client, to allow Ilse to help.

"I—I'm not crazy," Sam murmured.

Ilse looked up, but not over, though she could still track her client out of her peripheral vision. Eye contact could be perceived as a threat. She kept her gaze focused on the window, staring out at the lake. Again, Ilse said nothing.

Sam winced, inhaling shakily, her breath rattling in her chest like a wheeze. "I—I hate that I can't remember." For a moment her voice cracked, but then she hid it in a cough, choosing anger now. "I couldn't have been much older than seven, maybe eight…"

Ilse blinked now, her own memories surfacing for a moment. She pressed a finger to her maimed ear, but then lowered it again. Now her focus was on the client. On Samantha's emotions. Samantha's past mattered more in the hour they'd set aside.

"That's very young. Only seven or eight," Ilse murmured, simply mirroring back the words. Playing a role, though, repeating the thought aloud to prompt subsequent thoughts.

"I've lived in Seattle my entire life," Sam murmured, softly. She glanced at Ilse, now, watching the other woman for a moment. "There are more serial killers in the Pacific Northwest per capita than anywhere else. Did you know that?"

Ilse had known that, and her frown flickered. Just this morning, on the radio, she'd heard word of a body found off an old trucker's lane in the forest, near Seattle. Another serial killer, perhaps?

Take captive every thought... She shook her head. No sense allowing considerations of a killer to intrude. Her client needed Ilse's full attention. Serial killer or not, Ilse wasn't in the business of dealing with the dead victims of murderers. Rather, she specialized in the ones that killers left alive, whether on purpose or by accident.

"I don't like sleeping," Samantha said. "Or dreaming. I see him there. I always see him there. I don't remember what he did… Why I managed to escape." She shivered, shaking her head. "It's all so horrible."

Survivor's guilt? PTSD, clearly. Ilse considered each for a moment.

"And these memories," Ilse said, glancing over now. "They started surfacing in dreams?"

"Yes. Yes, horrible dreams. Bloody dreams." Samantha whimpered, pulling at the sleeves of her sweater and shaking her head. "My mother doesn't talk about it—she lies about it sometimes. But she always gets scared, quiet, when I ask her."

"Ask her about what, Sam?"

The woman shook her head, staring at the lake, her eyes wide, unblinking, fixated as if on something in the distance. "The abduction," she murmured. "How he took me…"

"You were only a child?"

"Seven, I think. Like I said, my mother lied about it." Sam turned to Ilse sharply, staring at her. "I'm not crazy!"

"I don't think you are."

"No, really, I'm not! My mother doesn't want me to think about it. She wants to pretend it never happened… But now… now I remember…" Samantha's voice squeaked and she swallowed, blinking back tears all of a sudden.

Ilse was careful with this next question. Too strong, and she might trigger the PTSD; too light, though, and she'd be of no help at all. "And you don't remember what he looks like?"

Sam froze for a moment, as if glued to her seat, her arms motionless, her fingers stiff against the cushions of the couch. "I try to," she said, her voice shaking. "I try…" She looked over, her eyes fixated on Ilse. "But no. I don't remember. Just glimpses and snapshots…"

Ilse smiled in a comforting, sad sort of way. She said, "I'm happy to help you remember, if that's what you want."

But the woman blinked, frowning now. "Remember? I—no, Dr. Beck, that's not why I'm here. At least, not completely."

Ilse didn't betray her confusion, keeping her expression docile. "Oh?"

"I'm here," she said, her voice rising in volume and pitch, anxiety and fear tinging her tone, "because he's still out there!"

"The serial killer who abducted you?"

"Yes! He's still out there. And he's re-targeting me! I know he is. I can tell." The breeze brushed the window and tapped lightly against the glass. But it might as well have been a gunshot, as Sam turned wildly, gasping and staring at the swinging frame.

Ilse reached up gently, wedging a book beneath the window, keeping it in place. Slow, careful movements. "You believe he's coming after you again? After all these years?"

Ilse pictured her own memories surfacing… More than two decades since that scene in the basement. Two decades, nearly, since she'd seen *him.* She shivered, but gritted her teeth, forcing her attention back to Samantha.

"I'm not crazy," her patient repeated. "I can… can *feel* it. Someone was watching me at the grocery store last week. It could have been him. I don't know—I ran."

"So you think he's coming back for you?"

The woman wagged her head, nodding. "Yes, Dr. Beck. I *know* it! I'm not safe. I need your help. To remember what he looked like—not to remember for remembering's sake," she swallowed, "but so I can protect myself. So the police can catch him. I know he killed people. I just don't remember how many, or who."

"Or what he looked like?"

Samantha shivered and didn't answer, pausing for a moment and rubbing at her elbows. She looked lost, tired, like a rabbit trembling in a hutch. Ilse's heart panged with compassion, but at the same time, her own troubled thoughts swirled.

Should she call the police? Was Samantha delusional? The fear seemed real. The dreams… the haunting thoughts returning seemed likely.

But the lying mother? The non-concrete details? Possible for repressed memories. Probable, even. Ilse glanced up at the clock. 9:58. She stared at the second hand, watching it tick by. The session ended at 10:00. Ilse felt a flicker of unease swirl in her stomach, staring at the second hand. 9:59. She winced at the number, feeling her fingers quiver. Ilse hated imprecise numbers—the way they hung suspended, like an unanswered question. One had to be precise with time. Imprecision bred anxiety, and anxiety compromised excellence.

She could feel Samantha's fear, feel her sense of defeat. It would perhaps be best to call the session.

But it was only 9:59. Imprecise.

The session ended at 10:00.

And so, in silence, she waited, watching the second hand like a runner waiting for the sound of a starter pistol. Ilse swallowed, dabbing at her lip with her tongue, breathing slowly, shallowly.

The second hand ticked past the twelve.

Ten o'clock exactly.

"I'm afraid we're out of time," Ilse said, exhaling in relief along with the words. Schedules had to be kept. Time mattered. Preciseness mattered.

Samantha seemed relieved at this declaration and she sprang to her feet, rubbing and twisting her hands in front of her, nodding in gratitude. "Thanks, Dr. Beck," she said, softly. "I—sorry I couldn't be more help. I—I just… I know he's coming. I can feel that he is. I need your help." Her next word came out strangled and desperate. "*Please.*"

Ilse rose as well, her features arranged in a comforting, conciliatory expression. She didn't touch her client, but swept her hand past the woman's elbow in a sort of comforting, patting motion, without actually making contact. "You have nothing at all to apologize for, Sam," Ilse said, softly. She gestured with a hand toward the door, nodding as she did. Exactly ten o'clock. She didn't have time to wait, though, as she had a meeting of her own at 10:30. She was going to be late if she didn't hurry. Then again, this case was fascinating and heartbreaking all at once. She could feel a swirl of compassion for this woman. At the same time, she could feel a sense of foreboding. She felt troubled, too…

So many of Samantha's disjointed, distant memories reminded Ilse of her own past… her own family… her father.

She shivered as her client stepped past, pulling her sweater tight around her, shoulders slumped, head bowed in a posture of defeat.

"I don't want to make you wait a full week," Ilse said, blinking and following after her client toward the front door of her home. "So how about tomorrow? Same time?"

Samantha's expression flushed with sudden gratitude and relief. She paused in the doorway, one hand on the brass knob. She swallowed, then nodded once. "Thanks. Really, thank you. All right, Dr. Beck. Tomorrow."

"See you then."

The woman's shoulders only seemed to slump further as she stepped out the front door, moving out beneath the gray Seattle sky. She pulled her arms tight around her, and then moved toward the Jeep she'd parked in the gravel driveway.

Ilse watched the woman leave, one hand braced against the door. She winced, still considering her own memories, rising, swirling to the surface. As she watched Samantha get into her Jeep, Ilse could feel tremors along the backs of her hands. She frowned now, and then murmured, "Bundy. Brown hair. Brown eyes. Forty-two. Thirty victims. November twenty-fourth. Forty-six." She listed the words quickly, precisely. "Antisocial disorder. Possible multiple personality disorder." Then repeated them. Slowly, as she did, her breathing regularized, and she began to calm.

The Jeep pulled out of the driveway, kicking up dust as it reached the road, and then pulled along the winding forest trail, away from the lakefront house.

"Dahmer. Blond hair. Ninety-four. Seventeen victims. May twenty-first," she recited from memory, rattling off the description. "Schizotypal personality disorder. Borderline personality disorder. Psychotic disorder."

Morbid though the recitations were, they helped calm her nerves. Helped her focus. And Samantha needed Ilse's focus—all of it. Was the woman delusional? Or was she right? Was a serial killer actually re-targeting her? If she was telling the truth, how had she escaped all those years ago, as a child?

How did you *escape?* a soft voice echoed in her mind. Ilse shivered once more, and shut the door to her home with a *click.*

She felt a tingle of anticipation, picking up her pace. If she didn't hurry, she was going to be late for her meeting.

CHAPTER THREE

Ilse moved back through the kitchen, pausing for a moment, standing next to her wood-burning stove. The faint scent of cinnamon and cranberries wafted from the oven. The granola she'd made the night before and left out to cool. It smelled nearly perfect.

No time to deal with it now, though. She left the oven door shut, and paused near a drinking glass in the dry rack. She frowned at the thing, certain she'd washed it the night before. But now, as she stared at it, narrowing her eyes just a bit, she could have sworn she spotted a bit of a fingerprint smudging the outside.

Running late for her meeting. But still…

She grabbed the cup, moved to the sink. Soap, water, rinse. Twice more. She stared at the glass, holding it over the sink.

Then she washed it again, just to be sure, before placing it carefully on the dry rack, wiping her hands off on the dish towel. She grabbed her keys from the counter, along with her wallet, and then turned, moving through the living room toward the front door. She locked, double-checked the locks, triple-checked the locks, then moved to the driveway.

She didn't pilot anything nearly so nice as a Jeep. But her Toyota Avalon was nice enough. She called it the Boat, on account of the size of the cabin and the faux wood trim circling the dash like the console of a pontoon.

As she backed out of the drive, she moved onto the dirt road lined by old pines and scattered with prickling leaves before picking up the pace. She lowered her window *exactly* halfway, fiddling with the controls a bit to make sure the glass perfectly split the frame. Then she allowed herself to relax, inhaling the scent of lake water and the odor of pine needles and dust.

In the distance, through the trees, she spotted the gray clouds pulling over the small town of Three Lakes. A couple of gas stations, a few supermarkets, and two diners served the small township. Though portions of the town lived on the lakefront, the denizens of Three Lakes weren't fond of attracting tourists. The lake community even had homeowners' association rules against Airbnbs.

The gloomy skies above watched the Boat maneuver along the pine-needle-strewn trails as Ilse made her way along the winding roads. Raindrops began to tap staccato against her windshield, pattering away against the glass.

Droplets of wet splashed through the open window, flecking Ilse's cheeks, and she allowed herself a soft little smile. Some people hated the rain—Ilse, though, liked nothing better. Florida and California could keep their sunshine; rain and clouds were more Ilse's speed. Rain would chase people indoors, clearing roads and sidewalks. Ilse liked the solitude.

She gave a soft little sigh of satisfaction, the water still pattering through her open window as she moved through the small town and pulled into the parking lot outside the nearest diner: The Seven Dwarfs.

She double-, then triple-checked the locks, before turning and, head ducked against the pattering rain, she hurried into the diner.

The restaurant was one of those that served everything and anything at all hours, with waitresses pushing sixty, at the youngest.

She paused for a moment, waiting for the host to return to his position behind the cash register. While she waited, her ever quickening thoughts darted back to the meeting with her new client.

Abducted as a child. A serial killer at large. Escaped before anything could happen. Foggy, hazy memories. Ilse winced—all of it was so similar to her own story. Spooky.

She shook her head, muttering beneath her breath, "Unknown. Brown hair, missing eye… Six victims. Still at large…"

"Becks!" called a voice from the far side of the diner, in a window booth.

A slender man with an impressive white beard was sitting straight-postured in the booth, waving her over and smiling. The host, who'd finally returned to the register, nodded in familiarity at Ilse. "Dr. Beck," he said.

"Hey, Horace," she replied, with a nod and smile of her own.

"Usual spot?" the man asked.

"Thanks," she returned.

Then she maneuvered through the tables, pausing for one particularly slow waitress to move past before joining Dr. Donovan Mitchell in the booth he'd reserved for them.

Dr. Mitchell wasn't just her own psychologist—as most therapists were in therapy themselves, and had their own shrink to mentor them—but he was also, in Ilse's case, a friend.

“Don,” she said, quietly.

“Becks,” he returned, patting a plastic hand against one of the place mats.

She glanced from his bushy white beard to the artificial appendage of his amputated arm. He reached up, delicately pushing with his prosthetic fingers against his glasses, moving them up his nose, and raising eyebrows nearly as white and bushy as his beard. “Good day so far? How was that reference I sent you?”

Ilse slid into the booth, huffing a breath and brushing her hair in front of her ear. “Fine,” she said, softly. “A strange case. Obviously I can’t get into it.”

Dr. Mitchell nodded, waving a finger toward one of the waitresses and flashing his million-dollar smile, causing his eyes to light up and the corners to crinkle. He returned his full attention to Ilse.

“I told you it was a peculiar one. I thought perhaps you’d be able to provide some insight.”

“I hope so,” Ilse murmured. “I’m seeing her again tomorrow.” She paused, considering what would be appropriate to share. Instead of asking directly, though, she said, “I’m trying to think of new ways to help some of my clients open up,” she said, softly. “Something to help them relax, and remember.”

“Relax and remember—a high ask,” said Mitchell. “Tried Seeking Safety? Or exposure?”

Ilse clicked her tongue and folded her hands on the table in front of her. “I’m not sure how effective cognitive behavioral therapy will be in these cases…” She pictured the woman’s frightened posture, the way she’d twitched at the slightest glance. Ilse’s own memories flitted up again…

A dark basement... scissors in her father’s hand. She glanced to the side and back at her mentor. Cognitive behavioral therapy hadn’t worked with Ilse either. Not before, and not now. Was this new client any different?

Again, she felt a jolt of discomfort at the sheer number of similarities between them, but she suppressed the thought and cleared her throat.

Dr. Mitchell leaned in, a light glinting in his eye, as if intrigued. “I see,” he said, his curiosity clearly piqued. “What about phase-oriented treatment of structural dissociation?”

Ilse gnawed on her lip. “I have no sense of dissociative disorder. Nor complex PTSD.”

Mitchell rubbed at his chin. "So no to the trauma model, no to cognitive behavioral therapy… What about medication for PTSD, maybe an SSRI?"

"Too early for any prescription."

"I see," said Mitchell, leaning back now, and yet somehow still maintaining his perfect posture. The man's slim frame was due in part to the three Ironmans he'd already completed in his seventies. He was training for a fourth, and Ilse knew the bicycle she'd spotted outside belonged to her old mentor.

"Well, Becks," he said, glancing up as a waitress approached, moving slowly through the tables, "likely we need more information, then."

Ilse wrinkled her nose at the pet name. "Likely. Mitch," she added.

It was his turn to react, raising his white eyebrows. "Mitch?"

"You call me Becks, I call you Mitch," she said, with a wink. "You know how I feel about the nickname."

Dr. Mitchell leaned in, smiling with his eyes, though his lips were drawn in a line. "Ah, but I don't know your real name, do I, *Ilse*?" His eyes flicked down to the tattoo on her wrist.

Ilse shrugged uncomfortably. Donovan Mitchell was the only person she knew who'd been smart enough to realize the moniker she used wasn't her given name. He didn't know her full background—no one did. But it was part of his charm that he never questioned her on it nearly so much as he looked for clues. Sometimes Ilse felt like he spent time with her simply to try and unravel the mystery of her past.

Other times, though, he simply seemed to like her company, and the ability to help her with any of her current clients. He'd been the first person to recognize the talent she had in the field—she'd only been a teenager at the time. He'd personally mentored her, and given her the recommendation that had gotten her into the program at the University of Washington.

Dr. Mitchell had been somewhat of a father figure in her life, and she could only thank him for it.

Then again…

She shivered as more memories surfaced. One hand probed up to her maimed ear.

Father figures of an entirely different sort haunted her dreams… Most of her memories from what she'd endured in that remote house, back in the Black Forest in Germany, had been repressed. Her past, similarly buried. Her other name, her background, her lineage, her history… All of it hidden, swirling around deep, *deep* down, where they'd been locked out of sight.

Perhaps that's why she wanted to believe this new client… Many of her clients who'd survived horrors didn't always make it. Some, though, managed to claw their way back to the light.

These success stories gave Ilse hope for herself. After a fashion.

"I'll try something else tomorrow," Ilse murmured, lost in thought as Dr. Mitchell ordered lunch.

This new client believed a serial killer was re-targeting her… Could the same thing ever happen to Ilse? She shivered at the thought… shivered at the flutter of long buried memories somewhere deep in her gut, and she folded her arms around her, feeling cold all of a sudden.

She'd need to do some research when she got home. Something to help her new client open up… The radio had mentioned something about a murder nearby on a maintenance road. Could that help ease into an exposure model?

First thing when she got home, she'd double-check the news. Maybe there would be something useful for tomorrow's session.

***

Ilse didn't have a smartphone. She didn't trust them. So, in order to read the article, she'd been forced to wait until she returned home to boot up her behemoth of a PC—nearly a decade old. This, coupled with the wood-burning stove and the analog clocks, was only a small part of her mini-revolt against all things overly technological.

She sat in front of the clunky, beige computer screen, her eyes narrowed as she scanned the article posted the previous day. The headline told the story.

Hitchhiker Murdered East of Seattle…

She scanned the contents of the article, her eyes flicking along the buzzing screen. She didn't like using computers too long—they always seemed to give her a headache. The article was sparse in detail, suggesting the local boys and girls in blue were playing things close to their vests.

She clicked off the screen, massaging the bridge of her nose, and shut down the computer. It would take ten minutes for the ancient artifact to boot up again.

Above her, she could hear the tap of droplets against the roof as it continued to rain into the evening. She got to her feet slowly, stretching as she shifted back and forth. She'd need to get some exercise in soon. She'd been a runner in high school and college, but had moved on to more practical forms of cardio recently, and certainly wasn't interested in competing in any of Dr. Mitchell's Ironman competitions. Rather, she preferred more practical forms of aerobic exercise. The gym where she trained, though, would be closed in the evening.

For a moment, standing in her lakefront home, with the sound of rain around her, she felt a jolt of loneliness. Ilse moved down the hall, toward the porch, standing with one foot inside the glass enclosure, and one back in the hall.

She peered out at the distant lake, at the mist curling above the water and the steady stream of raindrops disturbing the surface. The dark body of water beneath the evening sky, surrounded by old pines, reminded her of her youth back in the Black Forest.

An oddly familiar and disturbing setting. Ilse knew all too well she'd manifested a present setting where she couldn't escape her past.

Did she want to escape though?

Or remember?

A flash of scissors. An angry bellow in the room.

She still couldn't recall what had happened next. She reached up, rubbing at her maimed ear, tracing a finger along the scar over her cheek. Physical evidence helped fill in some of the blanks. But most of her memories…

Gone. Vanished like mist over the lake.

The loneliness settled on her shoulders just like the mist, low and thick and barely tangible. Perhaps she should call Mitchell. Maybe one of her friends from the gym? Her jujitsu instructor was usually up for sparring. Then again, she'd started to suspect he was simply hitting on her.

She sighed softly. Who could she call? She had colleagues, but not too many friends. Mentors, but not family.

Just then, Ilse's phone buzzed. She looked down, reaching into her pocket and pulling out the small TracFone. A dumb phone. No internet, no video—not even a camera. Text and voice only. Discardable, untraceable. The sort of phone drug dealers often used; pay as you go.

She lifted the device, realizing she'd been sent a voicemail.

Ilse raised the phone and listened, frowning. It was Samantha.

"Dr Beck!" the voice crackled over the speaker. *"I...I think I'm being followed. I—please! I need help. He's here. Oh God! He's... Wait... No. No, sorry. It was just the mailman. Sorry, Dr. Beck."* Some

heavy breathing, soft crackling, and the sound of thumping feet. And then, *"Sorry. I'll see you tomorrow, Dr. Beck."* A click, and then static.

Ilse sighed, lowering her phone, closing the flip lid and pushing it back in her sweatpants pocket.

The paranoia was far more deep-seated than she'd previously thought…

Unless it wasn't paranoia at all. Ilse frowned. What if Samantha was telling the truth? What if someone really was after her?

CHAPTER FOUR

Erica held her umbrella over her head, hunched over. She gave the front left tire of her old Camry a kick for good measure, muttering darkly beneath her breath as the rain continued to patter along the old road at the base of the mountain. The reaching pines and old trees shivered in delight beneath the droplets, the leaves shuddering and chortling on contact.

Erica glanced up and down the dark, worn, solitary road, and staring against the deluge for any indication of the tow truck.

"Come on," she muttered beneath her breath. "Where the hell are you?" She glanced down, fumbling with freezing fingers to pull her phone from her pocket. Keeping the umbrella upright and braced against one shoulder, she shielded the device, and as much of herself as she could manage, scrolling through the phone.

Nearly thirty minutes ago… Thirty minutes since she'd called the tow truck. She'd holed up in the back of the old Camry for nearly the full half hour, but had grown restless cramped in the back as she'd been. Now, though, circling the vehicle again, and stomping along the stray, damp gravel, she hadn't yielded much in the way of a new solution. She spotted the old, pink ice cream cake box in the back seat. Melting, no doubt. The small, little silver gift—an action figure—rested on top of the cake.

The tire was flat, and she had no spare. Only one other car had passed in the last half hour. She glanced over her shoulder again and peered down the meandering asphalt trail, breathing softly. She held the phone up, examining the reception.

Spotty at best. Triple A had said they'd be along by now. A curtain of liquid puddled from the edge of her black umbrella.

"Damn it," she muttered, glancing back down the road again.

Erica's lips trembled from the chill air, and her shoes and socks were already soaked by the puddles forming on the side of the road. She tilted her head and the umbrella just a bit to glance at the road moving up the mountain in the other direction, but there was no sign of traffic from that way either. Slowly, as she leaned against the driver's side once more, she paused, one hand reaching out toward the damp handle. Her fingers scraped against the metal, but before she could open her door and resign herself to another half hour of impatient waiting with a melting ice cream cake, she heard the squeal of tires and the wet whirring sound of rubber against asphalt.

She turned and glimpsed headlights arching over the incline. Erica's heart jolted in excitement.

She glanced at her phone for the confirmation message from Triple A, but it was quiet. Maybe the reception had prevented them from contacting her. She raised a hand, waving it past her umbrella, feeling the wet droplets against the back of her knuckles.

"Over here!" Erica called.

The vehicle slowed, the headlights even brighter now, blinding Erica for a moment as it pulled up behind her broken down Camry.

Erica's smile faltered a bit as she stared at the vehicle. She stepped onto the road just a bit, so the lights weren't so blinding. It wasn't a tow truck. No decal on the side. Not Triple A.

She frowned, stepping back toward the front of her car, feeling a faint prickle of anxiety mixed with hopeful relief. Maybe a good Samaritan had chosen to lend a hand. The front door of the truck popped open, and a voice called out beneath the rain, "Need some help?" It was a grating, painful voice, like some smoker from a commercial aimed at teens.

Erica hesitated, glancing back at her phone again. "I'm fine," she said, hesitantly. "I have a tow truck coming."

"You sure?" said the same rasping voice. "I have a spare, and a jack. Looks like you have a flat."

Erica felt a glimmer of hope. She glanced back at the ice cream cake. At the present on top. If she missed a birthday again, she knew her ex would bring it up in custody hearings. She felt a flicker of frustration and swallowed it back.

"You sure? I don't mean to trouble you."

"No trouble," the voice replied. "Just hang tight."

Erica moved around the side of her Camry, approaching the front of the truck.

She heard a soft *thump* as the driver hopped out of the car. The man had a low-angled hat, and he walked with a bit of a limp. He wasn't particularly large, and she glimpsed a scar looping around the man's left wrist, just above a glove.

He held a tool chest in one hand, and seemed indifferent to the rain.

"Oh, sir, here, let me help." She hurried over, extending the umbrella over her good Samaritan.

The man just grunted though; he hefted the toolbox and then cleared his throat. "You don't happen to have a lighter, do you?"

Erica coughed delicately, wondering if her car smelled of smoke. How embarrassing. "In the glove compartment. I've got it; one second."

She opened the front of her car, leaning the umbrella against the support formed by the top of the vehicle and the door frame. Then she inclined across the front seat, her legs still out of the car, the rest of her bent over as she angled her fingers toward the glove compartment. She winced, groaning at the strain as she opened the box and began to rummage around, looking for the lighter.

She heard the *thud* of what she guessed was the toolbox being lowered. Behind her, she heard movement, the scrape of something metal, suggesting the toolbox was being opened. She'd seen people jack up a car before, but figured it probably would be best if she was out of the vehicle when it happened.

Her fingers scrabbled against the green plastic of the lighter, and she pulled it free. At that moment, though, something fluttered past her cheek.

She frowned, reaching instinctively as if to swat away a mosquito. Except there, against her chin, next to her shoulder, she found a pink slip of paper. A Post-it note.

She began to straighten up. "What's this?" she began.

Before she had finished, though, she read the neat handwriting on the note. A small little smiley face adorned the top.

The note simply read, *Ten seconds left. Scream for me, please. I'm about to kill you.*

The raspy voice behind her murmured, "One… Two…"

Erica's emotions took a moment to catch up with her reading comprehension. And then, fear jolted down her spine. She began to whirl around, but at the same moment, someone slammed the front door against the back of her legs, buckling them. She yelled in surprise and felt her umbrella crumple above her.

"Three… Four… Five!"

She tried to whirl around but felt something against the back of her spine; a knee, pressing hard. Now, angled over her seat as she was, she couldn't move. She felt fingers against her lower back, moving up to her shoulder, as if someone were mimicking walking legs with their first two fingers. "Six… Seven… Eight…"

"Please," she gasped, helpless and trapped by the door and the knee, lying across the two seats. "Hey! Help!"

"Happy to," said the painful, rasping voice. "Don't struggle, I don't want to stain the seats. Also, nine and ten, by the way."

Erica tried again to whirl around, but again the knee shoved hard, painfully, and then something else, sharper, gouged into her neck from behind.

She yelled, gasping, and felt a sudden warmth along her throat.

Then it all ended.

CHAPTER FIVE

It was with some relief that Ilse Beck opened the front door to her new client. For a moment, as she stood there, one hand holding the door open, her eyes did a once-over, examining Samantha Wright. The blonde-haired, slump-postured woman had one arm tucked against her side, a pale hand holding her wrist in a defensive way.

But she seemed in good health. Ilse smiled pleasantly and stepped aside.

"Sam, good to see you. Come on in."

"Hey, Dr. Beck," her new client said, swallowing and glancing over her shoulder. Her Jeep was parked in the drive again, behind the Boat. "Sorry… sorry about the voicemail," she muttered. She didn't quite make eye contact, a flash of shame and frustration darting over her countenance, and then she sidled past Ilse, into the house, making a beeline toward the patio door which led to the glass-enclosed porch overlooking the gray lake.

Ilse closed the door behind them, double-checking, then triple-checking the lock, before following Sam into the makeshift office space.

She waited for Sam to choose a seat—the same one as last time, facing the lake—and then settled in the desk chair adjacent to the couch.

Ilse folded her hands across her lap and continued smiling pleasantly. "I'm glad you're back."

Samantha tugged at the edge of her sleeve, as if trying to pull it past her fingertips. She glanced uncertainly off to the side, swallowed, and looked back at Ilse. "I really am sorry."

"Nothing to apologize for. Fear can be crippling. Sometimes, though, facing the fear can help put it in its proper place."

Sam watched her warily.

Ilse pulled out the printed piece of paper she'd picked up from Donovan's office earlier that morning, extending it to her client.

Sam hesitantly reached out with pale, fragile fingers like delicate twigs, and accepted the printed paper, but before Ilse let go, she said, quietly, "Don't look at that just yet."

Samantha paused, one hand holding the paper, the text facing toward the floor, her eyes wary, fixated on Ilse. "I… What is it?"

"Have you ever heard of exposure therapy?"

"I… Maybe on TV. I don't know what it is though."

"Yesterday, you mentioned someone took you from your home."

"Kidnapped me," Samantha said, bluntly, her eyes flaring for a moment, her breath coming in rapid patterns.

"Yes," Ilse replied, smoothly, in a calming, normalizing voice. The gentler methods hadn't done much good the previous day. Of course, taking her time on a case like this was necessary, but on the other hand, Sam seemed genuinely terrified that someone was after her.

Ilse had to find a way to help. In the case of paranoia, to overcome or treat the fears. In the case of authentic memory, though… To help recover, and then notify the authorities about Ms. Wright's experiences.

Either way, taking things *too* slowly would only yield results like yesterday: confusion, fear, exhaustion. Taking things too quickly, though, could easily cause more damage, or collapse Sam under the weight of it all.

Exposure therapy didn't always have to target the original mode of trauma. Rather, adjacent exposures to minor and parallel triggers could often help.

"That," Ilse said, indicating the paper, "is an article from yesterday."

"An article?"

"A killer struck nearby, only twenty miles from here," Ilse said, wincing in a conciliatory way—communicating she was still on Samantha's side—but pressing on regardless. "Do you think you could read the first paragraph?"

"I… You want me to read about a murder?" Samantha shifted uncomfortably. "Why?"

"You mentioned the person who took you," Ilse said, quietly, "was a serial killer. You mentioned he harmed others, and you escaped."

"I only remember shadows of shadows," Samantha replied. "I don't remember much." Her fingers were now gripping the piece of paper tightly.

Ilse's eyes flitted from Samantha's pupils to her white knuckles, to her rigid arms at her side. Fingers enclosed over the palms—not aggressive, but defensive. Like embracing one's body to protect against an external threat.

Ilse watched her client quietly, considering if she should press further. Instead, she allowed her client to hold the paper, face down.

"I don't think I want to read about a murderer."

"You don't have to do anything you don't want to do," Ilse said, softly. "You mentioned you were from Seattle."

"Yes. So?"

"The murder took place only twenty miles from the city."

Samantha shivered. "Think it could be the same guy who took me?"

"That was nearly twenty years ago, yes?" Even as Ilse said it, her own spine prickled with fear. *Twenty years ago...* Hilda Mueller, in the basement, a hand clapped to her bleeding ear. Crying, crying. Her older siblings trying to shush her. Someone had hit her from behind, just to shut her up, to avoid attracting their father's attention. The sound of thumping footsteps.

Ilse swallowed, blinked, looked away, then inhaled deeply through her nose.

"Y-yes," said Samantha, softly. "Twenty years—it's a long time, I know. But he's coming after me again. I don't even remember what he looks like… but… but I do remember looking out a window," she said, swallowing. "I remember that. He… he would drive a red truck down the old road. I remember that too! But I don't know what he looked like. How could I not know!"

"I understand. It sounds horrible to not even remember what he looks like." Mirroring language. Allowing Ilse to recover, if only a bit, from her own memories. She shifted uncomfortably.

Sam shook her head. "I—I—and this article? You think it could help?"

"A killer striking nearby. A real threat…" Ilse shrugged a shoulder. "Maybe."

Samantha exhaled slowly, considering the words, staring at the paper, still keeping the text of the article face down.

Ilse just watched, waited.

"Twenty miles… that's close," Sam whispered. "Maybe it *is* him. Maybe he's targeting others… Did the victim look like me?" she said, suddenly, eyes on Ilse. "Did she have my name?"

Ilse just waited, allowing the considerations to do the work for her.

Sam shifted uncomfortably, the paper crinkling in her fingers as she leaned back. She still hadn't glanced at the text. But as she reclined, her eyes fixed on the lake through the window, her gaze became far off, her breath slow, labored.

For a moment, her eyes flickered, and her heavy breathing almost seemed to calm, in a sort of trancelike state. In a soft, probing voice, she murmured, "He locked me in the basement…you know. Me and the other victims. It was so dirty—smelled horrible!"

Ilse blinked. The mention of the smell caused more memories to play across her own mind. Memories of her own past, more than twenty years ago. Memories of the Black Forest—and the small house. A basement. Others trapped there too. Her siblings.

"He would hurt some of the others. Would hurt me too." Samantha sobbed suddenly, flipping over the page and staring at it. She blinked in confusion, glancing up. "This isn't an article," she said.

She turned the page to face Ilse. Indeed, instead of an article about a potential serial killer, it displayed text about a restoration projection for one of the nearby zoos.

"That's all right," said Ilse, staring at the paper. There had been no sense providing the actual document with the grisly details. Not yet, at least. Slow, incremental steps—that's what mattered.

"I… I remember something else," Sam said, suddenly. "I remember a strange rattling sound, like a flagpole out front. I remember screeching tires. My kidnapper would always leave in a hurry. Angrily. I could sometimes even smell the rubber. At least… I thought I could." She shivered and glanced off. The single piece of paper clutched in her hand fluttered to the ground like the final leaf shed in autumn.

Ilse just stared at Samantha. Her own memories swirled up in her mind. Twenty years ago, a brutal kidnapper, other victims… Hilda Mueller. Black Forest. The small house in the woods. Ilse shivered, but forced a calm, placating smile across her lips. She shifted slowly, trying not to show her own thoughts.

Ilse could feel a trickle of fear along her spine now. Not because of her own memories being stirred up. Memories prompted by the similar experiences of her new client. But a different sort of fear. A genuine fear, as if examined beneath a microscope and declared authentic.

She didn't think Samantha was paranoid. The memories seemed too real. The fear too real.

Which meant her client was telling the truth. She'd been kidnapped nearly twenty years ago, escaped…

And now she believed, it seemed, with all her heart, that someone was hunting her.

CHAPTER SIX

Agent Thomas Sawyer walked briskly up the mountain road, pushing his baseball cap back as he sidestepped the puddles in the trenches adjacent to the asphalt. His long legs stretched over the ground faster than his two babysitters with Seattle PD could keep up with.

He scratched at his chin, feeling six days of untended, and unintended, stubble along his jawline.

"Well?" called a voice behind him. "Agent Sawyer? What do you think?"

Tom paused by the caution tape, glancing from one of the orange traffic cones to another. He looked over his shoulder, expressionless, as he regarded Sergeant Alice Faber and her partner, Detective Robert Lopez.

They were neat, clean-cut, and well dressed in a city cop kind of way. For his part, Tom was wearing flannel, a baseball cap, and old, dusty jeans. He'd been stopped twice on his way up to the crime scene. Still, a small price to pay to avoid a suit and those infernal ties. Ties, in Tom's opinion, were like the flip-flops of the neck. Useless, dangerous, and—at worst—a weapon in a capable aggressor's hands.

Tom allowed the glance back to serve as sufficient response to Sergeant Faber's calls, and then, ignoring his entourage completely, he ducked under the caution tape, his eyes now fixated on the body next to the broken down Camry.

A couple of forensics people were making their way through the crime scene, murmuring to each other or going on their haunches to examine the vehicle or the corpse.

Before Sawyer got too close, he paused, indifferent to the eyes on him. He stood still, eyes closed for a moment, crossed himself, and offered up a small prayer his mother had once taught him. "Receive her soul, oh Lord," he murmured.

Then, still indifferent to the attention around him, he now focused, his gaze zeroing in on the body.

"Agent Sawyer?" came the gasping voice of Sergeant Faber.

This time, he didn't even afford her a glance.

"Excuse me, *Tom*!" she insisted.

He grunted.

"They haven't cleared the scene yet," Faber said, still breathing heavily. "Couldn't you wait just another ten minutes so the lab guys can make sure—"

Agent Sawyer glanced back at Sergeant Faber now, giving her a long look, and she trailed off with a frustrated little sigh. If stubborn had a color, it would match the green of Sawyer's eyes. His hair, on the other hand, was going prematurely silver. Though he was only thirty-five, the streaks of gray had moved from his temples and now dusted his hair, which he kept tucked beneath the Oakland A's baseball cap.

He tugged the brim of the cap, still not speaking. He didn't like speaking too much. Found it mostly a waste of air. Most of anything that needed saying usually could be communicated with action. And most of everything actually said usually could be left unspoken entirely.

Corpses, in Sawyer's opinion, were always more honest than people.

"Tom," Sergeant Faber said, jutting her lower lip beneath her pixie cut. "Can we just play nice for a few more minutes? Hmm?"

Detective Lopez was glowering over the smaller form of Sergeant Faber, his eyes fixed on Sawyer. Lopez had a square jaw and, Sawyer had been informed, was found handsome by most of the ladies in the department. The few times Agent Sawyer had worked with the locals, assigned by the Bureau office, he'd been paired with Lopez and Faber.

He didn't mind them. Though he suspected Lopez didn't share the sentiment, and Faber—while more patient—often got underfoot.

"No cigarette," Sawyer muttered.

"Ah, he speaks!" Lopez said sarcastically. "I was beginning to wonder."

Sawyer glanced back toward the car, back toward the body on the ground and the small green lighter which had been marked with a yellow number seven. He looked from the victim's fingers to the front seat of the car, then shook his head.

"What do you mean, no cigarette?" Faber asked, with a resigned sigh.

Sawyer waved a hand at the lighter. "No cigarette. Lighter wasn't for her."

Faber blinked. "Wait—you think the killer asked for a light?"

Sawyer adjusted the brim of his cap and began to stalk around the car in the opposite direction. He noted a couple other evidence tags by the side of the road, where wheel tracks scraped dust onto asphalt.

A couple of the lab geeks gave him a long look as he walked over what they thought was their crime scene. Of course, that was their first mistake.

The crime scene was no one's. Not yet. Not until the case was solved. And then Agent Sawyer felt certain *he'd* be the one to stake ownership. A suspect in custody as his claim.

"Agent Sawyer," Lopez said, making no effort to disguise his frustration. "Where are you going now?"

Tom, though, was moving toward the tracks on the road, frowning as he did.

"Sawyer!" Lopez said, louder.

Tom glanced back, raised a prematurely silver eyebrow. He pointed toward the road. "Killer's truck," he said. "Same tread."

Lopez blinked. "Same tread?"

Faber stood next to her partner, frowning. "As the other murder? The one from yesterday?" she asked.

Sawyer nodded. Faber was the smarter of the two. He liked smart. He addressed his next words to her. "Same truck. Same tread. Both necks slit." He shrugged. "Serial killer?"

He inflected it as a question. Lopez's frown became rather fixed at these words. The handsome, square-jawed detective glanced off into the trees for a moment, as if looking for a ghost.

"He's not still here," Sawyer said, feeling the urge to chuckle, but keeping his expression placid.

Lopez, though, wasn't entirely useless as a sleuth, it seemed, as he detected the humor. The man scowled. "Didn't realize they taught you BAU sorts how to track tread."

"Didn't learn that at the BAU," Sawyer said. "Learned it fixing trucks. All right—I've seen what I need to."

With that, he turned, marching back down the hill with Sergeant Faber and Detective Lopez sighing and moving after him again. He heard Lopez muttering behind him, quiet, but not so quiet he couldn't hear. "Is it true? Did he punch an FBI director in Oakland? I hear that's why his wife left him. I don't blame her."

Sawyer glowered, one hand rubbing at the knuckles on his left hand. Then he picked up the pace, marching back down the hill toward where the police cruiser was parked.

He'd volunteered for the case, of course. Perhaps things hadn't worked out perfectly with his marriage or last post. By the sound of things, the news was making the rounds even among those outside the

Bureau.

Then again, it had always been plain to Sawyer and his ex.

His first love, his first marriage, was to the job. Everything else took second place. He stepped over the swirling brown puddle on the side of the road, asphalt crunching beneath his boots as he marched on, considering the two crime scenes.

Both women were victims of opportunity. A premeditated crime, then, but not targets.

A killer looking simply to kill. Indiscriminately. He jammed his hands in his dusty jeans pockets, hunching his shoulders against a sudden breeze.

An indiscriminate killer meant they'd hunt again. Predators like this never stopped, not until they were put down. But such ambition took leg work. Good thing Sawyer had never balked at late nights or slow drives through mountain roads. If he had to comb every inch of the area himself, he'd do whatever it took for a bloodhound's whiff of the murdering bastard.

CHAPTER SEVEN

Ilse double- and triple-checked the locks to the front door. She waited, listening to the sound of the Jeep pulling away from the driveway as it moved on to the dusty road, slicing through the forest paths, away from the lake house.

As she stood there, Ilse breathed slowly, in and out. In her mind's eye, she glimpsed memories, shadows, attempting and threatening to surface.

"Doss. Eleven victims. Blackouts, depression. Poison."

But even the memory trick didn't serve to calm her nerves.

She glanced down at the tattoo around her wrist. *Take captive every thought.*

Sometimes it was easier said than done.

The sound of the Jeep had faded now. But the effect left behind still lingered. Samantha Wright had remembered *some* things. Remembered the trauma, the danger. Remembered, at least in part, what had occurred all those years ago, in the basement of the Seattle home.

Ilse shivered at the thought. It was all so eerily similar to her own past. Also twenty years ago. Also in a basement. In the Black Forest, in Germany.

Ilse shivered, shaking her head, standing by the door and closing her eyes for a moment.

And then she saw him.

The mismatched eyes, the scraggly beard, the sound of gristle crunching, and his bloody smile as he stared at her over the broken animal.

"See, Hilda," he had said, his voice raspy. "Do you see what can be done to something so small? You are very small too."

Hilda shivered, staring at the pigeon, now little more than a lump of meat and feathers in her father's hands.

She heard the rattle of the cage and glanced down. Another bird, flitting about behind mesh, metal bars. A bird purchased only that morning, purchased by her father. Briefly, little Hilda had thought perhaps her father was bringing her a pet. But of course, she should have known better. At least this time, he hadn't left it with his children for a week, allowing them to bond with it first. Perhaps he'd intended to, but had simply gotten too excited about the prospect of what he wanted.

"It's easy," he'd said. "See, just like I did. The neck is very fragile. Go on, now it's your turn."

Ten-year-old Hilda Mueller stared at the little pigeon glancing around from its perch in the cage.

Maybe it was looking for its friend. She glanced toward the broken mess on the table in front of her father, at the blood streaking his teeth.

"I don't want to," she'd said, pleading. "*Please*."

"Hilda," her father snapped, his voice turning to fury just as quickly as most people smiled. "Either you do that to it, or I'll do it to you!"

Ilse shivered, feeling tears coming down her cheeks, and she snapped back to the present, blinking aside the recollection.

The memory drifted away, back behind the closed door in her mind, where she had locked it away all those years ago. She opened her front door now and stared at the empty driveway, toward the old road meandering through the trees. She was safe now, though. Could the same thing be said for Samantha?

Ilse forced her mind to switch track, to allow the repressed memory to drift once more, flitting along, like seaweed drifting to the bottom of the ocean, buried by the deep in the dark.

Samantha, yes. Focus on her client. Focus on someone else.

With trembling fingers, she reached toward her mailbox, if only to have something to do. The memories, when they returned, sometimes came like a wallop to the chest. And sometimes they snuck up in dreams, robbing her sleep.

It had been years, though, since she'd collapsed under them. Years since she'd completely capitulated to the demands of terror.

Take captive every thought.

She began to sort through her mail, standing on the threshold, cycling from one bill to another. Junk, a local restaurant. And then…

She frowned, staring at a postcard.

It took her a moment, but then she stiffened. The rest of the mail fell from her hands, scattering across the ground like feathers from a bird.

She stared at the postcard, her breathing coming rapidly, irregularly.

She swallowed, unblinking

The postcard displayed a picture she recognized. A landscape photo of trees, and inclines, and mountains. Not so dissimilar to the surrounding area outside Seattle.

But this wasn't a photo of the Pacific Northwest. She didn't even need the cursive writing in the corner to tell her what the photo was.

The Black Forest. Germany.

She stared and flipped the note over.

Just two words. Nothing else.

Hilda Mueller.

She held the postcard as if it were glued to her fingers. At the same time, her vision darkened, narrowing, as if she were speeding up a tunnel. She trembled and shook, gasping.

Desperately, she closed her eyes, but the words echoed in her mind. *"Or I'll do it to you!"*

Now the pigeon was in her hands.

She could feel the eyes of her siblings around the room. All of them older. She'd been the youngest.

Their dirty features stared out from beneath greasy, unwashed hair. They barely moved, and they certainly didn't make a sound. None of them wanted to attract their father's attention.

"Hilda," he'd bellowed, "do it! Do it. Do it, like this!"

Large hands grabbed her small fingers. Large hands pressed hers against the bird's neck. Large hands squeezed until Hilda yelped from the pain of her own knuckles cracking.

Ilse snapped back again, gasping as if she'd just gone through a bout with her jujitsu instructor. She paused, bent over now, hands on her knees. Faintly, from the direction of the kitchen, she could smell the odor of cinnamon from the homemade granola.

Even more faintly, from somewhere up the road, she thought she heard some of the neighbors laughing. Was that the smell of a barbecue?

Her heart hammered now, and she glanced along the trail.

Hilda Mueller. Who would've known that? Not even Donovan Mitchell knew her real name.

She stumbled back in the house, shutting the door, double- and triple-checking the locks. Then she hurried over to the dinosaur computer. Her phone wouldn't help. So she had to wait almost ten minutes, waiting for the behemoth to wake up. The connection to the Internet was spotty at best, but there she sat in the chair, rigid, dutiful, waiting. And at last, the computer booted.

With trembling fingers, one hand still clutching the postcard, she used her other to type in the return address.

Who would know her name?

Was someone trying to contact her? One of her other siblings? Someone begging for help?

Could it be her father?

She shivered. Was he still alive? Most likely. Bogeymen never died.

Her fingers were still shaking as she typed in the return address.

Nothing. No results. A fake. An address for a local grocery store. Not an address from Germany. One from nearby. Only a town over, just outside Three Lakes.

Someone was taunting her with her past. And they were nearby.

Ilse cursed and got to her feet, checking the door's locks again, closing the patio door that led to her home office. The windows, she knew, were already secured.

She stood quiet, listening, waiting. As a child, listening had saved her life more than once. Inhale, exhale, slow. Try to suppress the fear. Try to move past it.

But how could she move past the fear?

She stood in her old, lonely lake house, with no one for company except for her memories, and a mocking postcard.

Was she overreacting? Was she being paranoid now?

She thought of Samantha. For a moment, she felt a flicker of sympathy. That poor girl. Was this what she'd been feeling too?

It was almost like fate had aligned, allowing her a slow introduction into glimpsing her past once more, through the eyes of a client. But that slow introduction was speeding up. Someone was nearby. Someone had sent her this postcard. Someone who knew her name.

Knew her past.

Was she overreacting?

Ilse felt a chill at the thought. She gritted her teeth against the memories like flickering shadows on a cavern wall. Someone from her past had found her.

Her frown deepened and her hand bunched into a fist. One way or another, she'd get to the bottom of this. Strangely, part of her felt a slow draw to her client. She needed to help Samantha. Her client was being hunted too. Dr. Mitchell often said the lives of his clients mirrored his own. Now, in Ilse's case, perhaps to a spooky degree.

Or, perhaps, fate had come calling.

She needed to help Samantha remember her kidnapper. In a roundabout way, Ilse felt certain this would unlock her own past. Unlock the source of the postcard. She nodded adamantly, swallowing once. With her help, Samantha would remember her kidnapper. They were going to find this serial killer. Not in some evidence lab, or at a crime scene. No, they were going to find a killer in nothing other than Samantha's own memories.

CHAPTER EIGHT

Sawyer glanced around the local precinct. Dingy, dark, a couple of sputtering bulbs over by the interrogation rooms. He felt a hand nudge at his wrist, and glanced down to see Sergeant Faber pushing a small, prepackaged sandwich against his fingers.

"Come on, Tom," she said. "You haven't eaten all day."

Sawyer nodded his thanks and took the sandwich, though he had no intention of eating the thing. Not now, not yet. Not while he was still focused.

"Can I get those files printed?" he asked, glancing back.

Detective Lopez, who was standing within earshot, snorted. "Do it your own damn self, *Agent.*"

Sergeant Faber, though, just nodded and moved quickly off toward her desk. Sawyer didn't acknowledge the sneered comment by the block-chinned detective. His mind was already flitting from one crime scene to the next. The same tire treads. Same execution style.

Both of them victims of opportunity, but premeditated crimes.

He settled slowly at the empty desk the locals had provided for him, and, checking the coast was clear and Faber was still by the printer, he tossed the plastic-encased ham and cheese and wet lettuce into the trash can.

He thought better while hungry anyway.

Faber returned a moment later, placing the two printed files in front of him. "Need anything else?" she asked, her pixie-cut hair outlined against the sputtering bulbs over the hall behind her.

Sawyer grunted in response.

The paper was still warm from the printer as he lifted it and narrowed his eyes, examining the files. The first victim: Sarah Beth Yount. Only twenty-one years old. A runaway turned of age on the lam. Throat slit in the forest off a trucker's lane.

He looked at the second sheet of paper, studying this next picture. Erica Cline. Twenty-eight. Divorced, dealing with a rough custody hearing, by the looks of things. Sawyer winced, briefly grateful that he'd never had a kid of his own with his ex. What a mess that would have been. Even in the driver's license photo, Erica had bags under her eyes.

Now she was inside a bag, somewhere kept cold, waiting for the autopsy.

He frowned at the thought, tapping a finger from one picture to the other. Both of them in their twenties, both of them within a twenty-mile radius of Seattle. One of them a hitchhiker, the other with a car. One of them from the right side of the tracks, another from *under* the tracks. No connection apparent at first glance. Different races, different appearances.

Truly victims of opportunity then.

"Lopez?" he said, calling over his shoulder.

The man didn't reply right away, though Sawyer could see his reflection in the monitor on the desk next to him.

Sawyer waited a moment, and Lopez blinked first. "What?" snapped the detective.

"How late is that curfew?"

"In the area where we found the victims? Ten. What are you thinking, Tom?"

"Patrols?"

Lopez narrowed his eyes. "I don't speak grunts and inflections. Patrols *what*?"

Sawyer turned now. "You guys sending additional patrols?"

Lopez crossed his arms over his neat outfit. "We'll be patrolling the area. Yeah. Got an idea what this bastard looks like?"

Sawyer paused, glancing at the printed photos, picturing the crime scenes in his mind. Both of them women, both of them small, young. Both of them had trusted the killer enough to allow him close.

"Non-threatening appearance," Sawyer murmured. "Under the age of fifty. Right-handed."

"Middle child?" Lopez scoffed.

Sawyer shook his head, ignoring the sarcasm. "Don't know yet." He returned his attention to the files, frowning even more deeply as he did.

No sense telling the locals the obvious. No need getting them jittery for patrol.

But it was clear as writing on the wall.

Even with the local PD out in full force tonight, even with the curfew, eyes couldn't be *everywhere.* Unless they got a lucky break, there was a good chance someone else would die tonight.

Sawyer got slowly to his feet. He hated desk work, hated desks on principle. He stared at the two printed sheets, glancing from one victim to the other, eyes narrowing.

"I'll join the patrol," he said, glancing over his shoulder. "I'll use the unmarked. Thanks, Faber," he added, nodding at the sergeant where she stood off to the side beneath the flickering lights.

Nothing he could do just sitting around the precinct. Nothing he could do until they had more information. The killer was out there. Besides, it didn't take much of an excuse to entice Sawyer away from a desk in a dingy office space.

He was meant to be on the move. Perhaps he was married to the job, but if that was true, no one could ever accuse him of unfaithfulness. A couple of loops along the same mountain paths where the killer had been lurking. Maybe he'd get lucky tonight.

CHAPTER NINE

Ilse reached for her old, dumb flip phone on the nightstand, unable to fall asleep—haunted by Hilda Mueller. Haunted by the postcard. Maybe she should call Dr. Mitchell—someone else. She shifted on her bed, but the moment her fingers made contact, the phone buzzed and she jerked with a surprised yelp.

Her hand retracted automatically, and she stared the buzzing phone, swallowing hard. She reached out trembling fingers in the dark of her old lake house, and took the phone in hand. Lifting it slowly, she answered, "Hello?"

"Dr. Beck?" said a voice on the other line.

Ilse went still. Samantha again. Her new client. She felt another jolt of selfish thinking. Samantha's case was too much, triggering Ilse's own memories. Maybe she ought to drop her as a client.

No. She couldn't. That wasn't what Mitchell would have taught. It wasn't what Ilse knew was right.

"Hello? Ms. Wright?" Ilse said, keeping her tone even, calm. "Is everything okay?"

"Y-yes. Sorry, Dr. Beck. Is this a bad time?"

Ilse hesitated. She glanced around the room, ignoring the postcard. Then she got up and moved out into the hall, walking slowly with bare feet against the wooden floorboards toward the glass patio.

"No, no, of course not," Ilse said, softly. "How can I help?"

"I—I've been remembering things. I did what you said. I read about the murder yesterday. There's been a second one, Dr. Beck. A second!" Samantha's voice creaked suddenly, and a whimper crept into her voice, which she swallowed back with a big gulping breath.

"Yes, I heard about it on the radio," Ilse replied quietly. "I didn't mean for you to go reading about it on your own. It was just an attempt to jog memories. It might not be wise to keep—"

"But it worked!" Samantha said, excited on the other end.

For a moment, Ilse frowned. She thought she could hear the sound of crunching footsteps through the phone. The sound of labored breathing.

"Are you at your home?" Ilse asked.

Samantha brushed off the comment with a grunt. "Couldn't sleep. I went for a walk. But look, Dr. Beck. I—I think I may have remembered where I was kept!" The excitement in her voice was palpable.

Ilse reached the glass patio facing the lake. She stared through the dark trees beneath the night sky. Her eyes fixed on the gloomy water. Another wave of rolling mist had spread across the lake, filtering through the trees to marry the lake homes in shadow.

"Where you were kept? When you were abducted?"

"Yes, Dr. Beck! I saw it briefly. It was a memory where I felt so scared. So very, very scared! But I allowed it to play out. There was an old, abandoned shack. I think it was on a farm, Dr. Beck! I saw a farm. Are there any farms near Seattle?"

Ilse frowned. "What type of farm?"

"There was a rusty, bent weather vane of a rooster on the shack… But the type of farm? I—I don't know… Is that bad?"

"No. You're doing wonderfully. All right, so you saw an old shack. A farm. Do you remember what color the barn was?"

"Red—I think… Or, well, maybe… No, I think I'm making that up. I don't remember the color. It was old, though. Very worn out. I do remember that. Because I remember thinking about my Uncle Sal's place in California. How he'd been forced to renovate the whole thing. Cost him nearly as much as a new house."

"An old, worn down barn, then?"

"Yes!" More excitement and a louder crunching sound, suggesting Samantha had picked up the pace of her nighttime stroll.

Ilse felt a shiver. The voice on the radio announcing the second murder had confirmed Ilse's suspicions that a serial killer was on the loose. Samantha suspected her own captor was coming after her again.

"You're outside?" Ilse said.

"Yes, Dr. Beck. Don't worry, it's just the bike path behind my house. Look—I was thinking about the farm. I… I think maybe I'd recognize it if I saw it again."

Ilse felt her pulse quicken as more mist rolled in over the old, gray lake and through the dark, looming trees. She could hear Samantha's labored breathing. Could hear the sound of her brisk walking.

For a moment, Ilse wondered at her own boogeyman. Who had sent that postcard? Her father? Very possibly. If so, how had he found her?

No, not her father. Dr. Mitchell. Yes. Must have been. He was a clever man, very clever. She wouldn't have put it past him, from their conversations, to have put it together. Ilse didn't have an accent anymore. She hadn't gone by Hilda Mueller in more than twenty years. But she was sure there were hints. Psychological tells and tips that Mitchell could have put together over the last fifteen years of knowing her. He'd trained her.

Yes. It must have been Mitchell. A tasteless way for him to reveal his discovery. Then again, he wouldn't have known about the surfacing memories. About the pigeon in the cage. The scissors in her father's hand. Those horrible mismatched eyes.

Ilse shivered, her fingers pressing hard to the phone, holding it to her cheek. Her eyes fixed on the lake through the patio windows.

"Where are you?" Ilse said, suddenly. "You know to stay away from Dubuque Road, right?"

"I… Wait, what? Why?"

Ilse felt a flicker of fear. "You're not near there, are you?"

Samantha swallowed on the other end. The sound of footsteps faltered for a moment. There was only quiet, and then, "I live near there. My house is at the foot of the mountain, right next to Dubuque Road. Why, Dr. Beck?"

Ilse felt a flicker of worry. "How far did you read those articles, Sam?"

"Just the first paragraph. Like you said!"

"Sam, listen to me. You shouldn't be out and about now. Not there. That's where the killer has been—"

"Hang on, Dr. Beck. One second." Samantha's voice increased in volume, but then muffled as if the phone had been lowered from her cheek. "Hey!" Samantha called, clearly addressing someone else. "Careful!"

Ilse heard the sound of gravel, and tires against the road.

"No—no!" Sam's voice grew suddenly louder.

"Samantha?" Ilse said, sharply. "Samantha!"

Ilse heard a sudden scream. The sound of a slamming car door, hurried footsteps, and another strangled yell. And then the line went dead.

Ilse stood in her lonely lake house, staring out at the gray waters, her eyes unblinking, fixed on the mist. She swallowed, listening desperately, hoping beyond hope for the line to connect again. But all she could hear was silence.

CHAPTER TEN

Ilse's silence didn't last long, and action soon followed.

The first sound was the steady *thump* of rapid footfalls against floorboards. Then came the sound of jangling keys where they were snatched from the dish by the door. Last came the sound of the locks on the front door. Double-, then triple-checked.

Finally, Ilse raced out to the Boat, ignoring the sense of the night surrounding her. Ignoring the oppressive, cloying weight of darkness on her shoulders, the mist over the lake curling toward the house in wisps like the fingers of a ghost.

She flung herself into the front seat of the old Avalon, breathing heavily. One hand jammed the keys into the ignition. But then she paused, staring at the house.

Had she locked?

A small, niggling itch in the back of her mind. The compulsion. Had she locked the door? What if it wasn't locked. Was it locked? Had she locked? Was it locked? Had she locked? What if the door—

Ilse cursed, got out of her car again, sprinted to the front door, checked, and checked again to make sure. Locked.

She felt the inevitable surge of relief. Dopamine centers rewarding her for giving in to the compulsion. Then she raced back to her car, put it in gear, and tore out of the driveway.

Dubuque Road. That's what Samantha had said. She'd gone for a walk on the old biker's trail next to the mountain.

Ilse knew where that was. She sped up the road, her eyes fixed on the path ahead curving and curling through the trees beneath low-hanging boughs and branches, through the swirling mist and past the gray waters.

She should have listened to her client. Listened to her instincts. But instincts were tricky, untrustworthy. Instincts were costly. Facts. History. Repetition. These things could be relied on.

In this case, though, she'd been distracted.

By her own thoughts. Her own history.

A little postcard with two words: Hilda Mueller.

Ilse ground her teeth, pulling her phone from her pocket, her eyes still glued to the road. She only spared the faintest glance to find the three numbers.

9-1-1.

***

Agent Sawyer could feel the boredom pressing in. He circled the old trails by the logger lanes and old trucking roads for the tenth time in the last hour. No sign of idling vehicles. No shouts. No instances of hitchhikers or joggers ignoring the curfew. He'd spotted a couple of kids throwing bottles at a tree, but one quick whir of the siren in his unmarked sedan had sent them scramming.

As he took the mountain path again, the car angled up, climbing the old road, his eyes fixed off into the distance, his mind working through the sparse information he'd been given on the case.

No viable connections between the victims.

Victims of opportunity in a premeditated killing spree. What did that tell him?

Agent Sawyer was a man who trusted instinct. Instinct was like the snuffling nose of a hound on the track of scent molecules. Instinct was what gave him the edge—gave the BAU the edge. Granted, not all of his colleagues or higher-ups saw eye to eye with his methods.

It was why he'd been restationed, after all.

He frowned, recollecting Detective Lopez's biting words. *"Is it true? Did he punch an FBI director in Oakland?"*

Sawyer massaged his jaw briefly, running a rough, calloused finger along the edge of his chin. He stared through the fogging windshield as he wound his way through the mountainous roads. Absentmindedly, he lowered his hand, his knuckles trailing along the buttons of his flannel shirt. He tilted his head, feeling the plastic strap of his baseball cap pressed to his prematurely graying hair, and puffed a little sigh.

The way his knuckles pressed to his buttons aroused a familiar sensation. He could still glimpse the image in his mind. Glimpse the way he'd lost his temper, jolting across the table, hand swinging before he'd even realized what was happening.

Sawyer shivered at the memory, puffing another breath, fogging the glass from the inside this time.

Certainly not his finest moment. Lucky he hadn't ended up behind bars.

Only his prior relationship with Director LeGrange had kept him from more serious consequences. Still, a six-month suspension, and then a transfer up to this gloomy place. It wasn't like LeGrange hadn't deserved it. Sawyer already knew, if he ever saw the director again, he'd punch him a second time for good measure.

But as far as consequences went, things could have gone worse… far, far worse.

He'd lost his only friend with that punch. Lost his wife not long after. He could still feel the hot jolt of fury. Feel the rage bubbling up. Could see the way his old director had frowned, tensing at the look in his eyes.

Sawyer thought he'd had his temper under control. He was a man governed by instinct, but also a man who could keep his temper in check.

Or so he'd thought.

Until he'd heard the news… until the director had told him.

Sawyer sighed, shaking his head and gripping the steering wheel. No sense dwelling on the past. He was in Washington state now. Still BAU. Still doing what he was meant to.

Silver linings could be found even in the overcast Pacific Northwest.

As his thoughts meandered, trailing along with the crunch of the tires against old roads, his radio crackled to life from his dash.

Sawyer straightened a little, grateful for the distraction from rumination and boredom.

He answered. "Yeah?"

"Tom?" said a voice. Sounded like Faber.

"Hmm?"

"Hey, we just got a call," came the voice over the radio, full of static and hesitation. "A young woman was attacked on Dubuque Road. She was on the phone when it happened."

Sawyer perked up. "Where?"

"You're out by Three Lakes, yeah?"

"Driving by it now."

"Well, it's near to you. Already have a couple of cars heading over. Detective Lopez should be there first. Thought I'd give you a heads-up."

Sawyer twisted the steering wheel and faced down the mountain, picking up speed and flooring the gas. "Where again?" he called, sharply.

"Sending coordinates now. Check your cell phone," came Sergeant

Faber's voice.

"Mhmm," he replied. He clicked off the radio, feeling his cell phone buzz and pulling it from his pocket. He tipped the brim of his baseball cap back, frowning at the GPS coordinates sent his way, and then angled the vehicle down the slick mountain road, picking up speed as he headed for the location.

Sawyer inhaled the perpetually damp mountain air through his open window, eyes on the road ahead, but mind projected even further. He liked to take problems as they came; one step at a time. But he could feel those steps quickening, the pace picking up. He didn't smile, but he felt tempted too.

The hunt was on.

The first sign of anything awry was the flashing blue and red lights beneath the dark gray skies and reflecting off the overhanging leaves on dew-tipped boughs. He pulled sharply over to the concrete barriers off the side of the road, jolting out of his vehicle as he did in one swift motion.

He didn't even remember to slam the door as he hurried over toward where a group of police officers were standing by the concrete barrier near a jogger's path and bicycle trail.

He recognized Detective Lopez standing furthest along the dirt road, under the trees, flashlight in hand, aiming it up and down.

Raindrops still clung to some of the leaves, but mercifully, though the skies remained overcast, the deluge had subsided.

"Anything?" Sawyer called, drawing near.

Detective Lopez glanced back over the concrete barrier, still in his suit and tie. He wrinkled his nose as the flannel-and-ripped-jeans-wearing BAU agent drew nearer. Then he gave a very Sawyeresque grunt. Participating in conversation without actually volunteering anything. Minimal effort.

Maybe Lopez wasn't so bad after all.

The detective nudged the wet road with one foot and spread his hands, waving them up and down. "Apparently call was coming from this trail," he said at last, a grudging note to his tone. "Haven't found anyone."

"Crank call?"

Lopez shrugged. "Didn't seem it. Was some shrink—her client or something. She was on the phone at the time. Heard an approaching car, then a scream or something."

Sawyer nodded, already moving along the trail, fishing his phone from his pocket and clicking on the light.

He aimed the flashlight off the side of the trail, moving with long steps away from where the whirring blue and red lights and gathered police were waiting, surveying the side of the road.

Sawyer walked a distance, but then pulled up, frowning. If the potential victim had heard the sound of an approaching vehicle, then that meant she'd been near enough to the road. He turned back, heading in Lopez's direction once more, his eyes off the side of the trail, frowning as he did. He briefly considered what someone might do when accosted by an unfamiliar party.

Stay on the trail?

Maybe. But what if the aggressor was faster?

His eyes slipped from the dirt jogging path toward the undergrowth and scrap on the side of the road now, surveying every inch he could discern.

He faced the detritus, feet set. Then he stepped sideways once, paused, examined, and repeated the motion.

"What the hell are you doing?" Lopez called.

Sawyer ignored the detective. He took another step, then stiffened. Immediately, he dropped to his haunches, probing with his cell phone light toward water-dappled leaves and, there, the glint of something metallic.

He leaned in and then straightened again, lifting a cellular device.

"What's that?" Lopez said suddenly, his tone shifting.

"Phone," Sawyer replied. He grunted, and then glanced toward the leaves again, waving a couple of fingers. He felt a prickle in his chest, and a sudden weight in his stomach. "Blood," he added, pointing toward the leaves.

He paused long enough to cross himself, using his own phone. He offered up a quiet little prayer beneath his upturned baseball cap, eyes closed as he faced the canopy. And then he returned his attention to Lopez.

"Did you say blood?" the detective asked.

Sawyer nodded silently toward the crimson-speckled leaves, hefting the phone in one hand. Cracked. Out of battery too, it seemed.

At that moment, as Lopez edged in, calling for one of the uniforms by the concrete barrier to come as well, there came the sound of screeching tires.

Sawyer frowned toward where a sedan was pulling in along the shoulder, behind the two squad cars and Sawyer's own unmarked vehicle.

A Toyota by the looks of it. Old, well-maintained. Maybe belonging to some older married fellow?

He blinked when he spotted the woman scrambling out of the front seat, breathing heavily and brushing her hair on the right side of her cheek. She brushed it forward instead of back. Strange. The woman was wearing sweatpants and an unflattering baggy gray sweatshirt.

She moved toward the police officers by the barrier, but was intercepted by two of them, who held out their hands and began a murmured conversation.

The woman fidgeted uncomfortably, and Sawyer watched as she glanced toward her vehicle, then held up an apologetic hand and hurried back over, testing the handle as if to see if it were locked or not. She checked the door twice, before emitting a soft little sigh of relief and returning to the police officers who were watching her with mounting curiosity.

The woman looked to be in her early thirties. She had arrived at the scene in a hurry, but seemed in control of her emotions and had calmed enough. Even though Sawyer couldn't quite make out her words from this distance, he could tell she was speaking in a controlled way.

Sawyer sighed, then passed Lopez, slapping the recovered and cracked cell phone into the man's chest. The detective frowned at the handling of the evidence, but before he could protest, Sawyer passed by, stepping with one long leg over the concrete barrier and approaching where the two police officers were talking to the strange new arrival.

The woman glanced past the police as Sawyer drew near. She took in his baseball cap, his flannel shirt, and the frown on his face.

"Hello," she said, quickly, redirecting her words toward him. "I'm Dr. Ilse Beck. I'm the one who made the call."

Sawyer glanced back over his shoulder, then returned his attention to the woman. He just waited, allowing the silence to prompt further information.

"I… She was on the phone with me at the time," Ilse said, hesitantly, her eyes searching, gauging, adjusting. She had an intelligent, analytical gaze. "Is—did you find her?" At this, her voice cracked a bit, and some of the calm facade faded to reveal a mixture of fear and… was that guilt?

Sawyer frowned. "How'd you know the victim?"

"So she is a victim?" Ilse asked.

“Found her phone. Found blood,” Sawyer said, shrugging once.

One of the officers eyed him for a moment. Likely not impressed by Sawyer’s decision to share information with a layperson. Then again, if this woman was the last person to speak with the victim, she might prove useful.

“Blood?” Ilse said. She pressed a hand to her lips, holding it there for a moment, her eyes widened in horror. She let out a strangled little sigh that turned into a sob. Sawyer felt a flesh of sympathy, but swallowed it back. Commiseration would only distract now. A life was on the line. Besides, he was a good judge of character, and unless he was completely wrong, Ilse was a tough nut to crack.

She glanced off for a moment, staring up the mountain road, then returned her attention to Agent Sawyer.

“I… I think I know who might have done this,” she said, her voice hoarse.

CHAPTER ELEVEN

Ilse could feel the gaze of the baseball cap–wearing cop fixated on her. He hadn't introduced himself yet, but she could tell he was in charge, simply by the way he moved, the way he held himself. He had an air of authority, but also one of distance from the other police gathered.

Not a cop, then? A federal, maybe?

She shook her head, nibbling on her lower lip and feeling a swirl of guilt and anxiety flush through her system.

Samantha had been taken. Her phone discarded, blood on the trail.

Ilse bit her lip hard, feeling a jolt of pain. She could feel her own anxiety rising, swirling, she wanted to scream, to yell. But for the moment, she kept her posture calm, docile. She kept her eyes fixed on the tall, silver-haired man in the flannel shirt.

"What relation did you have with the victim?" the man said, speaking in a slow, even-paced way. He had an air of unhurried competence about him. No panic, no rush, just confidence born of competence.

"I'm Samantha's therapist," Ilse said, quickly. "We were on the phone only twenty minutes ago. I called it in when it happened. Is—she's not—is she…"

"No body," the man said, simply.

Emotionless, straightforward, minimal words. Ilse cataloged this information as well, piecing together what little she could about this person. "Are you FBI?" she asked suddenly.

The man blinked as if in surprise. He glanced toward the police she'd been talking too as if wondering if they'd told her. He looked back at her. "BAU," he said. "Behavioral—"

"Analysis Unit, I know," she said quickly.

"Agent Tom Sawyer," he said.

She blinked. "Tom Sawyer… As in?"

He sighed. "Yes. As in. Parents were readers. Look, Dr. Beck, you said you knew who did this. Well?"

She cleared her throat. "Ah, yes, well, Agent Sawyer… I…." She trailed off, running over the options in her mind. She couldn't betray client privilege, but she'd be an imbecile not to help find Samantha. She worried at her lip, feeling her teeth hard against her mouth. She should have listened to Samantha. She'd thought at first the woman was paranoid. Thought she'd been overreacting. She'd thought, at first, this had simply been a case of repressed memories and emotions surfacing and manifesting.

But Samantha had been clear; she had said someone was following her, stalking her. The same killer who'd kidnapped her when she'd been a child. The same man who'd gotten away with it.

Ilse stared off for a moment, feeling another jagged stab of fear and pain. She should have trusted her client. They'd only had two sessions, but Ilse should have called the police. She shivered, swallowing, feeling her own emotions rising.

Had she neglected her responsibility because of her own memories surfacing? Samantha's story had triggered Ilse's own past. Had brought to the forefront long since discarded and buried recollections.

Ilse wished desperately she'd talked to Dr. Mitchell. To someone, a colleague, or anyone about Samantha before… before *this.*

She glanced past Agent Sawyer toward the trail, her eyes staring at the dirt road where the silhouettes of other police had gathered. One of the cops was bent by the side of the road, examining something.

She shivered. A phone. *Blood.* That's what Sawyer had said.

"How much blood?" she said, her voice shaky.

Agent Sawyer pushed back the brim of his baseball cap, eyeing her. "Not enough to think she's dead," he said bluntly. "Probably struck or cut. Subdued. Killer didn't move the other two bodies," he added.

Ilse let out another shuddering sigh. She pictured her own boogeyman. Pictured the small house in the Black Forest, back in Germany. Winced, thinking of how horrible it would be if her father showed up all these years later. Snuck up behind her, struck her with a bottle or some branch… Dragged her off to a new lair.

Even as she thought it, she could feel her terror mounting. She could only imagine how horrified, how terrified Samantha was feeling now. Imagine how lost, in pain, desperate…

Ilse shook her head, staring at Sawyer. "I don't have a name for the guy. Don't even have a face," she said, simply. "And I can't tell you everything my client and I discussed, but I can tell you she thought she was being stalked. Being hunted by someone from her past."

"Stalked?" Sawyer said, frowning. His young features beneath prematurely silver hair made his face stand out like moonlight beneath cloud cover. The slight wrinkling of his brow wasn't so much a gesture of emotion, but rather one of instinct. This, she determined, wasn't a face accustomed to the wiles of emotion. He spoke in monosyllabic words, short sentences, lending the silence and his piercing gaze to communicate on behalf of his lips.

"Yes," Ilse replied. "Stalked. She claimed she was abducted as a child."

"Abducted?"

"It was never reported. She said she was abducted, and said the man who'd abducted her was a killer."

Sawyer's frown darkened even further. For a moment, he glanced off toward one of the parked cars, his eyes trailing to the trees and the old mountain roads. "Have you heard about the murders nearby?" he said, softly.

Ilse winced. "Do you think it's connected?"

Instead of answering her, he turned toward the police officers. "Expand the search," he murmured. "Report to me if you find anything."

"Sir," said one of the officers, "Detective Lopez asked us to stay here, to watch the road."

"And I'm saying expand the radius. Call it in, get more boots on the ground. Anything at all; report to me."

The officers shared a look, glancing back to where two silhouettes were moving about the trail. But then they nodded and began to move, one of them reaching for his radio, the other stalking toward the old dirt path.

Agent Sawyer glanced at Ilse. "I need you to come with me. That's my car. Think you can follow back to the precinct?"

It was the longest sentence he'd uttered since she'd shown up, and now it was Ilse's turn to simply respond with a gesture; a quick, nervous bob of her head. She brushed her hair past her ear and then began to move along with Sawyer, both of them hastening toward their vehicles.

Ilse sighed as she unlocked her car, sliding into the front seat and turning on her headlights. She should have listened. And now that she hadn't, now that she'd second-guessed, Samantha was out there somewhere.

Back in the hands of her old captor?

Ilse winced. She pictured the postcard that had shown up on her doorstep. Pictured her own memories rising to the surface. The soft feathers of the pigeon beneath her fingers. The hard, calloused fingers of her father's hands over hers.

She grimaced against a sudden *crunching* sound as Agent Sawyer pulled from the shoulder, his lights flashing across the asphalt road as he began to drive away. He made no effort to slow down or make it easy for her to follow.

She found herself breaking speed limits as she followed the unmarked car off the shoulder, up the road and back in the direction of the city.

***

Ilse sat hesitantly in the cold interrogation room, her fingers clasped delicately over each other. The scar from her ear and along the side of her cheek itched, but she resisted the urge to reach up and scratch it, lest she bring unwanted attention to it.

She swallowed, watching Agent Sawyer where he spun his own metal chair around and sat in it backwards, folding his arms across the backrest and fixing her with a piercing glare.

"Am… Am I a suspect?" she said, hesitantly, glancing around the cold, unadorned room. No two-way mirrors. No mirrors at all. Just a table, two chairs, a light fixture, and a sealed door.

Sawyer watched her for a moment. "You're a therapist?" he said. By his tone, he didn't sound much impressed.

"Yes," she said, slowly. "I work with survivors of the people you put behind bars."

He nodded once, his tongue inside his cheek as if tracing the inside of his mouth. He cleared his throat, glanced at his fingers as if thinking, then looked up at her. He didn't say anything.

She shifted uncomfortably, put off by the silence, by his watchful, searching gaze. At last, she spoke into the stillness. "I can't tell you much about her," Ilse said, softly. "Personal details fall under privilege."

"How about dead clients?" he asked, emotionless.

She frowned. "I'm trying to help. Doing my best. Her name. I can say her name. Samantha Wright."

Sawyer glanced down at a little notepad, scribbling in it with an old, worn yellow pencil. He looked up, waiting, as if prompting her to continue.

"That's all I can give. That and anything pertinent to the crime itself," Ilse said, insistently. "I've told you all I know."

"Samantha Wright?" he said.

"That's right. That's her name."

This time, he pulled out his phone, typing. He paused a second, then lowered his device next to the notepad.

The way he sat, backwards in the chair, baseball cap tipped up beneath the bright lights, flannel, buttoned shirt, like some old-fashioned western cowboy, plus his dusty old blue jeans made him look more like a farmhand or some laborer than a BAU agent. Even when he'd entered the precinct, some of the locals had given him long looks. He'd ignored them mostly.

Now, though, he wasn't ignoring her at all. His eyes seemed a spotlight, fixating on her. Or, perhaps, more like needles, pinning her to a page, like a butterfly with pierced wings; some sort of specimen.

She fidgeted uncomfortably.

"No," he said.

"Excuse me?"

"You're not a suspect," he said.

She frowned at the delay in the comment. He was watching, studying her. Almost as if he'd only just now reached that conclusion. Not because she'd said anything, or he'd looked up any details about her. Almost as if he were going off of gut instinct alone.

She frowned at the thought. If Samantha was in the hands of some maverick agent, maybe it was best she stick around. But what more could she say? What more could she add that was helpful?

Before she could speak, Agent Sawyer's phone vibrated once. The man's eyes darted to it like a hound spotting movement in the underbrush.

He cleared his throat, pressed a finger to the phone, then his eyebrows flicked up, a second later joined by his eyes which pierced her once more.

"Fake name," he said.

Ilse blinked. "Excuse me?"

"Samantha Wright. Fake name. No records. No social security number. No address." He gave a little puff of breath as if he were tired. "No social media accounts."

Ilse frowned, but only for a moment. Then she nodded once. She felt a twist of unease in her belly. A fake name… Like Ilse Beck? Like her own situation. She shivered, hoping this Agent Sawyer didn't dig too deeply into her own background.

"I see," she said, quietly. "It isn't uncommon, Agent Sawyer, for survivors of trauma to change their names in order to start their lives over. I've had other clients do the same." She trailed off, but then added in a ghost of a whisper, wincing beneath the bright lights of the interrogation room, "Especially if they believe their tormentor is still out there."

"Witness protection?" Sawyer said.

She blinked. "I—I don't know anything about that."

He sighed, crossing his arms and stowing his phone once more. "Just a possibility, I guess. Look, Dr. Beck, *anything* you can tell me might help. I know you think you're doing right by your client, but what good is privileged information if Samantha is dead, hmm?"

"Agent, I promise you, if I thought I had anything useful, I'd tell it to you in a heartbeat. I want to help Samantha as much as you. That's why I'm here. I… I think she's still alive. She has to be. Why would her abductor take her to another location otherwise?" Ilse nodded more for herself than anything. She needed to believe Samantha was alive. She had to be.

Sawyer inhaled through his teeth, wincing for a moment as if against a sudden cold. "Bit of an impasse here, then. She's a ghost. No records. Nothing. Can you at least tell me where she lived?"

Ilse paused. "I don't know that."

"Anything you got for me, Dr. Beck?"

"I wish I could. Really. I'll help however I can."

He sighed in resignation. Closing his eyes for a moment, he said, eyes still closed, as if he were in a bad dream, "Think you could stick around for a bit, then? You want to help. Something might come up. Something that jars that memory… and conscience of yours. Something that might get you to remember something useful."

"I'm happy to help in any way I can," Ilse said, reflexively. How could she refuse? She'd already failed her client. Already held on to information for too long, toeing the line between responsible and negligent as best she knew how.

And now, her client was gone, abducted.

And it was Ilse's fault.

She had to make it right. She had to help however she could.

But how was that, exactly?

And how could she help before it was too late for Samantha?

"I'll help in whatever way I can," Ilse repeated, more firmly. "Just tell me what I can do."

CHAPTER TWELVE

They no longer sat in the interrogation room. Ilse felt like that room was much like Agent Sawyer's personality. Rigid, cold, straightforward, and uncomplicated at first glance.

Now, though, they were in a break room, with two vending machines against the wall; one filled with energy drinks and the other with small snacks pretending to be healthy. Agent Sawyer had a thin, wiry physique, suggesting he likely didn't partake in either. Or eat much at all. He had a firm, dogged look in his eyes were he stood across from her, refusing to sit, leaning against one of the vending machines and watching her quietly, waiting.

For her part, Ilse's eyes were half hooded; she stared into the reflection off the glass of the vending machine, cycling through the notes she kept for her clients.

She didn't write the notes down. Not like Agent Sawyer in that little notebook of his. Rather, she cataloged them, memorizing them and placing them like building blocks in her mind. She thought of the memory device as an apartment complex. Each floor housing certain, organized memories. She could sometimes take the elevator, moving swiftly from one floor to the next, sifting through recollections. Other times, she took the stairs. A slower, weightier venture in knowledge retention.

Now, she moved along the imagined pathways of her mind, moving through the two sessions she'd had with her client. She swallowed once, and then, uncomfortably, beneath the watchful gaze of Agent Sawyer, she mimed reaching out with her hand. In her mind's eye, following a path of hypnagogic imagery, her fingers closed on the imagined door knob. She could almost feel how cold it was. She mimed, above the table of the break room, turning the door knob.

She pushed it in.

Organized, sorted, arranged. The memories of the two sessions came flooding back. She watched them play out, picking up on marker moments—shorthand more than anything—for recollecting rapidly. An eidetic memory. Not so much for facts and numbers, but for words and faces. For emotions, especially.

Sawyer cleared his throat, but Ilse ignored this gentle jostle.

Instead, she closed her eyes fully now, sifting through the memories of their last session.

Samantha had apologized at the start of the meeting. Marker one. Shame. She had then moved into explaining her reasoning. Marker two. Justification. She had continued into holding the piece of printed paper. Marker three. Courage.

And then…

Then she'd remembered. Bits and pieces. Fragments. The sorts of memories Ilse kept in the basement of her mind, unsorted, hidden, lost and buried.

But now, in this case, Samantha's own worn thoughts were kept cataloged in Ilse's mind. She watched in her mind's eye, picturing the frown, the grimace, then the words.

Even as Ilse played it out, she knew the clock was ticking. Time was running out. Samantha was out there somewhere, in horrible danger. She pictured the young woman's slumped shoulders, bowed head. As if the weight of the world, like Atlas, had fallen on her back to bear, with no one to help. The late-night phone calls, clear cries for help. The desperate, wide-eyed, nostril-flaring panic. Fear at its root.

Ilse opened her eyes, exhaling shakily, feeling a lance of guilt, of fear herself.

But then, softly, quietly, her voice like the mist so often over the lake behind her house, she said, "She mentioned… At one point, during a session, she mentioned…" Ilse paused—would this be appropriate to share? It had to be. She pushed on. "She mentioned she would sometimes watch out the tiny window in the shed where she was kept, looking for her tormentor's old red truck." Ilse shivered, a flash of her own memory. A dark basement, not a shed. The sound of tires—not from a truck, but still, similar enough.

Ilse sighed shakily, pushing aside the distracting memories. Her own thoughts, her own pain wouldn't help her. No, this was about Samantha.

Ilse delved back into the cataloged memories, the recollections of her sessions. She nodded slowly, doubling down on the words. "A truck, a red truck," she said. "That's what she said he drove. Nearly twenty years ago now… but still…" She trailed off, eyes open again, looking at Sawyer. She winced. "That's all I remember. She…" Ilse's voice cracked. "She said it would fill her with dread when she saw that truck coming down the road."

Sawyer watched her, not quite frowning, but not smiling either. His posture guarded, arms crossed, legs braced. His shoulder pressed against the cold surface of the vending machine. For a moment, his eyes flicked down toward where Ilse's hand still hovered over the table, mid-motion where she'd playacting the movement of opening an imaginary door.

With a delicate cough, Ilse quickly lowered her hand to the table, laying it flat.

"Red truck?" he said, his tongue circling the inside of his cheek again.

"That's what she said."

"She say anything else about this man?"

Ilse winced. "We were still working on that. It was hard for her to remember."

"Twenty years is a long time."

"People like their trucks," Ilse said, shrugging.

"It's a long shot."

"I'm sorry. Really, it's all I can remember."

Sawyer glanced at her hand again, and then he frowned. "You sure? Don't need to check your notes or anything."

Ilse didn't blink. She was used to people being skeptical about the memory devices Dr. Mitchell had taught her. But she knew they worked. They always had. It was one of the reasons clients often referred others to her. They felt known, remembered. Something so small as recollecting the name of someone's grandfather, or the color of their favorite pet. Paying attention to what others valued, and holding onto that information, helped open more doors than any amount of training she'd received.

"The killer… He's likely in his fifties now," she said, slowly. "Abusive, closed off, neurotic and narcissistic personality disorder," she rattled off, nodding to herself. "He lives in the area, or at least the surrounding area. Drives a red truck, or did."

The BAU agent quirked an eyebrow. "We'll see. All right. Thanks, Doc. I'll phone it in and see what hits. Check it out myself."

Ilse glanced out the break room window at the dark sky of night's crescendo. She frowned and said, "Are you heading out again?"

He was already moving toward the break room door, and waved a hand at her. "You're free to go, Doc. I've got it from here. Thanks again."

She got quickly to her feet, clearing her throat expectantly.

For a moment, she wasn't sure he'd look back, but he seemed to pause in the door and sigh, his shoulders falling just a bit. He glanced back at her, raising an eyebrow for a question.

"I'd like to come with you," Ilse said, crisply. She didn't look away, didn't blink. No weakness. Not now.

"Not possible."

"I'd like to come with you."

He waved it away. "Against protocol."

"Sharing client information is also against protocol except in the rarest of occasions," she said, quietly. "What if I remember something else? I can still help."

He puffed a breath, staring at her. Then he turned, walking off without replying. She watched him leave, frowning. He got to the end of the hall before finally raising a hand and giving the faintest of flicks with one finger.

Ilse didn't particularly like being gestured at like a puppy called to heel, but she was more worried about her client than her pride in that moment, and she hurried up the hall, her footsteps tapping as she pulled her arms in her sweater around her in the chill air of the precinct and followed Agent Sawyer back to the sliding glass doors which led once more out into the night.

A red truck. A man in his fifties. A serial killer who'd been operating for more than twenty years.

Time was running out. The clock was ticking.

CHAPTER THIRTEEN

"You sure?" Agent Sawyer murmured as Ilse watched from the back passenger seat. She stared at the side of his face, breathing softly, waiting to watch his normally expressionless face and try to pick up clues like crumbs from a table.

"All right, thanks," Sawyer murmured. "Just the three, you're sure?"

She heard the buzz of a voice on the other end of the phone, but then Sawyer just grunted once and hung up.

Ilse leaned in from the backseat, still watching the side of the FBI agent's face. He'd refused to allow her in the front seat, next to him. She felt like a suspect in the back, her arms braced against the seat. But again, Ilse had swallowed her pride. Samantha needed her, and she wasn't about to be distracted by the strange idiosyncrasies of an agent who'd never learned to play nice with others.

Besides, it wasn't like Ilse didn't have oddities of her own.

"So?" she pressed, when he volunteered nothing further. "Any more leads?"

"Three more," he said. "Fifties. Red truck. Twenty years local."

"Only three?"

"In the area. Three."

"Those last two weren't great," she said, and then wished she hadn't. Words for the sake of words. Somehow, it felt like Agent Sawyer dragged it out of her, as if she were trying to compensate for his own apparent bankruptcy of vocabulary.

Still, the last two houses they'd stopped at had been duds. First one, the man had died of a heart attack the previous year, but it hadn't been reported. The second, the man had been in a wheelchair, and no longer owned a red truck. His license had been revoked on top of it all, and he'd yelled them off his property at such an early hour.

Not an ideal start.

Ilse puffed a little breath and she could feel Agent Sawyer's eyes on her, watching her in the rearview mirror. She brushed her loose hair past her ear and settled in, watching the road beneath the dark as Sawyer maneuvered them outside Seattle once more, along old mountain roads.

Dawn hinted itself across the horizon now, and the overcast skies had cleared a bit. Exhaustion weighed on Ilse's limbs, on her eyes. She winced against a jolting headache, but swallowed, inhaling for a moment and staring at the sky to gather herself. A tinge of gray still made itself known on the horizon, wreathing the distant mountains, but at least the rain had stopped, though the roads were still darkened from damp.

"So three left?" Ilse said, doing that thing again where she filled in words for silence.

"Not great leads," he countered. "One of them lives in a nursing home now, just owns the property but doesn't live there."

"What about the other two?"

"One doesn't own a red truck. Blue, but not red."

"Did he used to own a red truck?"

"Wasn't clear," Sawyer replied, and added nothing further.

"And this third lead? What about him?" Ilse felt her own anxiety mounting.

In answer, though, Sawyer pulled off the road all of a sudden, onto an old dirt trail, leading past a mailbox shaped like a beehive with a little green flag.

"Is this it?" Ilse said.

"Third lead. Hang on—road's washed."

Even as he said it, Ilse's teeth jarred, and she winced as they bumped over the road. She rubbed at her neck, leaning back in the seat and peering up the road in the direction of an old house on a hill. "Is this it?" she said.

Sawyer's eyes narrowed, staring ahead, swallowing softly. "This is it," he said. "Yeah. Last chance."

"What about those other two leads?"

"Nah," he said, simply.

She frowned at the back of his head. "What do you mean?"

He shrugged. "They don't feel right."

"Hang on, *feel* right?" Ilse said, shaking her head. "No, look, just because someone owns a blue truck now, doesn't mean they didn't used to…"

He cut her off. "Call it gut instinct, Doc. They don't feel right. Hang on."

This time she was ready, and braced as the car jounced through another weathered portion of muddy road. She could see the way he was tensing now, the closer they got to the old house on the hill top. They passed a cleared section of woods, and she spotted an old stone well.

Sawyer seemed on edge. He was poised in a way he hadn't been on the previous leads.

"This might be nothing," she cautioned quietly.

"Feels right," he murmured back.

She wasn't sure what to make of this. Instinct alone was a poor law enforcer, as far as she saw it. Instincts had to be trained. Senses and feelings were useful insofar as they partnered with data, facts, and, especially, training.

"There are a lot of red trucks in a wider surrounding area," she replied quietly.

He glanced back. "Mhmm." Still, he seemed on edge, fingers around the wheel. His eyes were on the old house fully as they pulled off the muddy, worn road and slid up the trail, coming to a halt behind an old, weathered red truck.

Tom Sawyer got out of the front seat and moved around the side as Ilse exited also. Without a word, he held up a hand and frowned.

Ilse paused, staring at him.

"Stay in the car," he said, frowning even more deeply now.

She hesitated, one hand braced against the roof of the vehicle. "I—what if I can help?" she said, hesitantly. Her exhaustion from earlier was still swirling, and—perhaps—clouding her judgment. But Samantha was missing. She needed to help find her. In any way she could. Besides, sleep-deprived courage was as good as the real thing.

"You're a civilian," he said, firmly. "Stay in the car."

She glared. Then, pulling his own trick, she didn't say a word, and instead slammed the car door, crossing her arms and glaring.

He studied her for a moment, but then massaged the bridge of his nose and shrugged. "Fine," he muttered. He reached out, despite himself it seemed, to help her over a pool of mud.

His arm felt corded and firm beneath his flannel shirt, and his hand guided her, against her elbow, surprisingly gentle as he helped maneuver past the mud and dirt. Once they reached the patio, though, he let go immediately and gave her a firm look.

"Let me do the talking," he said. "And if I say get, you get."

"I'd like to help."

"No woman's car here," he said, shrugging once and glancing toward the drive. "Just the truck. Suspect's here alone."

"Suspect? He's not a suspect yet—is he?" She decided not to object to his comment about the truck either.

"Help by not slowing me down, Doc."

She inhaled slowly, glancing from the red barn, to the red truck, to the old house. Ilse shivered and stepped back, gesturing toward the patio steps and the worn blue rail.

She watched as Agent Sawyer stepped onto the porch, taking the steps two at a time, and approached the front door. He didn't knock first, but instead sidled along the window, glancing through a gap in the curtain beyond. For a moment, he stood, inhaling softly through his nose, one hand moving to the holster at his waist.

He seemed more poised, attentive, than he'd been at the other houses.

Gut instinct. *Doesn't feel right.*

She could only hope the strange agent's *feelings* didn't get anyone hurt.

At that moment, as Sawyer raised a hand to knock against the door, it suddenly opened inward, and a bright orange light was clicked on, flooding the entryway and casting a long shadow out across the patio.

A man in a dusty shirt stood framed in the doorway. A sudden loud barking echoed out into the night, and the man's thick leg blockaded what looked like a couple of pit bulls who were snarling and slobbering and growling in the direction of the folks on their porch. The man in the overalls blinked blearily, glaring out onto the patio, one of his hands tucked just behind the door frame.

Sawyer seemed to note this hand out of sight and frowned, his own fingers gripping his holster.

"Federal agent," Sawyer said, quickly. "Are you Mr. Campos?"

The dogs were barking even louder now, straining behind their owner's leg. The man in the door had a round beer belly, bare and visible over the edge of tattered, dirt-splattered jeans so wrinkled they looked like they'd likely been slept in for the last month.

Behind him, Ilse spotted an old, run-down couch, with all manner of bottles scattered across the ground, and wedged in gaps of the furniture itself.

The dogs barked even louder until Ilse's head hurt. She watched Sawyer stand, calm, cool, collected, one hand on his holster, the other cautioning toward Mr. Campos.

"Who's asking?" the man declared, his voice like a trumpet in the still dawn.

"Agent Sawyer, FBI. I need to speak with you, Mr. Campos. Please keep your animals restrained."

"You threatening to shoot my dogs?" the man demanded, jutting out his chin and his beer belly. A bit of spit seemed to have dried across his chest, along with the contents of one of those bottles behind him. The man's eyes were ringed red, and he winced against the faint rays of sun over the house.

"Keep your hounds back," said Sawyer. He didn't have a note of fear; rather, his voice carried a strange inevitability, as if he knew what was coming, but had to playact the buildup anyway.

"Get off my property!"

Sawyer reached slowly into his pocket, pulling out a badge. "FBI," he said, enunciating slowly. "Keep the dogs back, and come out." He seemed even more poised now, his legs braced, angled, his hands steady, his eyes fixed on the potential threat.

"Get off my property!" the man in question screamed. "And take that little bitch with you!" He waved toward were Ilse watched from the bottom of the patio steps.

Ilse stared at the man. Slovenly, drunk. The bottles on the couch suggesting he'd chugged through the night. The barking hounds, clearly pent-up, exhausted. Likely hadn't been walked or run in weeks.

She eyed the man's drooping belly over the edge of his overalls. Eyed the truck, covered in dust sitting by the front of the house. Truck didn't look like it had been out that night.

Neither did the man.

He was in his fifties, most likely. But other than his belligerence, he didn't strike Ilse as *off* in the sort of way she'd grown used to. Scores of clients. Survivors. Her own background, her own history with a certain *type* of person.

She knew the type all too well.

And this wasn't it. This wasn't a sadistic killer.

"I don't think—" she began to say.

But then Mr. Campos tried to slam his door. In response, Sawyer reached out, wedging it open with one foot. The drunken man yelled incoherently, and then lowered his foot, kicking his dogs in the ribs to propel them forward.

The animals snarled and jumped.

Calm as ever, Sawyer moved.

In one swift motion, he shoved with his foot, sending the lead dog backwards into the first with a snarl. In the same motion, he grabbed

Mr. Campos by one overall strap, yanking the man out onto the porch. He spun around with the man, flicking the door shut with the back of his heel as the dogs lunged again. This time, they slammed into the door as it also closed.

Mr. Campos took a wild swipe at Sawyer. But the baseball cap–wearing agent avoided the blow easily enough, as if sidestepping a breeze. He moved quickly, tripping Mr. Campos and then easing him gently to the ground.

The old man struggled and tried to kick again.

"Stop," Sawyer said, simply, stepping back and away from the drunk. Minimal damage, minimal pain, minimal harm.

And yet, in those three, swift movements, the dogs had been contained, trapped in the house, and Mr. Campos had been removed from where he'd likely stowed a gun behind the door frame, and at the same time, Sawyer had escaped unscathed. Ilse felt her jaw unhinge, her eyes widening. She swallowed once, quickly closing her mouth.

Still calm, barely breathing heavily at all, as if he had simply gone for a stroll, Sawyer stooped down, his motions still oddly gentle in contrast to his blunt demeanor. He fished handcuffs from his jeans, clicking them despite Mr. Campos's loud protests.

"Apologies, sir. But I need a word," Sawyer said, simply. Then, dusting off Mr. Campos, he helped the older man back to his feet, avoiding a headbutt in the process.

Sawyer gripped the belligerent drunk beneath the neck, pushing his head down and then leading him toward the stairs.

Only then did he glance over the man's hunched, blustering form and nod past Ilse toward the car. "Mind getting the door?"

She stared at the strange agent and swallowed once, clearing her throat. "As long as I don't have to sit in the back with him."

Sawyer paused, considering this. Considering it *far* too long in Ilse's assessment. But then he sighed in resignation, nodding once, before guiding—more than pushing—Mr. Campos toward the waiting, unmarked sedan.

CHAPTER FOURTEEN

Agent Tom Sawyer was in no rush as he reclined in the chair across the table. Back in the same interrogation room he'd used with the doc. He could feel her eyes on him, though he couldn't see her behind the one-way glass.

Ilse Beck. An unusual woman. And beginning to be a nuisance. He glanced toward the mirror where he'd allowed her to stand, watching. He had half a mind to send her home. But in the end, he'd decided her expertise might be useful.

Not that he trusted it.

Therapy. Just another word for jawing about one's feelings.

Fat good that did for anyone. So much navel-gazing people's eyes got crooked. Still, she'd been the one to provide the insight that had led to the arrest of Mr. Campos.

The man in question was still in his dusty shirt, still slick with sweat and the odor of stale beer. His eyes were hooded and narrowed, fixated on Agent Sawyer across the table. The large, round-bellied man had already staked his claim to the interrogation room with the half-hearted gob of spit he'd launched across the table.

Agent Sawyer hadn't blinked. He didn't blame the man. Didn't even dislike him. Like or dislike had nothing to do with the job. An arrest couldn't be made personal. That's when things got screwy.

"Did he punch an FBI director in Oakland?" He winced at the memory of the question and refocused his attention entirely on Mr. Campos.

Again, he maintained his silence, just watching, waiting. Word salad didn't do much as far as Sawyer was concerned. Better to let them sweat, to let them fill in the blanks themselves. Nothing was so horrible a questioner as one's own imagination.

And so he allowed the imagination to run wild. Granted, where Mr. Campos was concerned, it was probably more like a steady stroll with all manner of aching knees and huffing breaths.

"Imma sue your ass," Mr. Campos said at last.

Sawyer stuck his tongue in his cheek, but didn't say anything. Didn't bat an eyelid.

“Just watch,” Mr. Campos said, twisting his lips back in a snarl, much like his pit bulls, and revealing yellowed teeth. “Imma sue your ass. I’ll have your badge.”

Some detectives and agents liked to lead up to the questioning portion of an interrogation. Sawyer preferred to shoot straight.

“I’m here about a missing woman,” he said, simply.

Mr. Campos stared at him, his bloodshot eyes widening in his stubble-covered face. The man had so much fuzz it even went up his cheeks, bristling out from sun-stained skin. A flicker of… *fear*? Was that surprise? Sawyer frowned.

“I ain’t snatch no woman,” he retorted.

“You have an assault charge,” Sawyer replied, just as quick.

“That charge was withdrawn!”

“Did you threaten your ex? Is that why she took it back?”

“Pshaw. That shit was six years ago. Don’t you have better things to do than keep hassling?”

“Did you kidnap someone last night?”

Mr. Campos blinked at the straightforward question. He spluttered, then shook his head wildly, his jowls swinging. “Hell no! That crazy whore say I did?”

“We haven’t been in contact with your ex-wife.”

“I didn’t kidnap no one,” the man insisted. “Imma sue you.”

“Mhmm.”

Suddenly, Sawyer heard a quiet tapping sound on the door. He frowned, cleared his throat, and began to speak, but the tapping became more insistent. He sighed slowly. “One moment,” he said, holding up a hand toward Mr. Campos. He rose to his feet and moved to the door. He opened it a crack, frowning at where Dr. Beck stood in the hall.

His silver eyebrows shot up. “Yeah?” he said, slowly.

“Sorry, Agent Sawyer,” Ilse whispered, quickly. “Only, you said to let you know if I picked up on anything.”

“Mhmm.”

“Well…” She continued to keep her voice low, shifting uncomfortably from foot to foot out in the hall and wincing as she did. Sawyer sighed, tilting his head, the lights above and behind casting the brim of his cap across his features as shadow.

Ilse leaned in, cupping a hand over her mouth and whispering. “I don’t think it’s him, Agent Sawyer.”

She leaned back, nodding quickly to affirm her own words.

Mr. Campos was too busy leering over Sawyer at Ilse to notice she'd gone to bat for his bottle-swilling self. Sawyer puffed a breath, ejecting any burbling negative emotion along with it. No sense making it personal, not now, not ever.

"That's your professional opinion, is it?" he said. He made no effort to lower his voice. Instead, he glanced back at Campos. "This woman you've been ogling thinks you're innocent, Mr. Campos."

The man blinked again at the comment. Clearly, whatever he'd been expecting, it hadn't been this. He coughed delicately, clearing his throat on what was likely phlegm due to acid reflux and one too many brews. "I—well, yeah. I didn't kidnap no one!" he repeated louder and nodded fervently.

Ilse shifted uncomfortably and crossed her arms. She began to lean in again to whisper, but Sawyer just turned. "You wanna say something?"

She hesitated, glancing uncertainly from Sawyer to the suspect. "Would you like to step outside?" she asked, delicately.

Sawyer just shrugged. "You don't mind, do you, Mr. Campos?"

The man blinked.

Sawyer said, "See, he doesn't mind. Shoot."

"Umm. Well…" Ilse shifted uncomfortably, no longer glancing in Mr. Campos's direction. "I—just…"

Sawyer waited, lips pressed, unblinking.

"I just…" She glanced through the door again, then back into the hall, insistently, waiting for him to catch the hint.

But though he caught it, he dropped it and just waited. "Hmm?" he said.

At last, with a frustrated sigh, she murmured, as softly as possible, "It's not him. It can't be."

Mr. Campos had gone still too, holding his breath so he could hear, his chest motionless all of a sudden, the reflection from his slick sweat no longer moving up and down with his steady breathing.

"How so?" Sawyer said, making no effort to lower his voice.

"I—I mean…" Ilse glanced at Mr. Campos. Quickly, like ripping a Band-Aid, she said, "Look at him. He was drunk when we found him. He's clearly in no shape to be chasing young, athletic women down through the woods. One look at him, and Samantha would have run. There's no way someone with his… particular physique could have caught up." She held up a placating hand toward the overalls-wearing man but then returned her attention to Agent Sawyer.

"He's too fat to kill?" Sawyer said, summarizing.

Mr. Campos narrowed his eyes, and Ilse shifted uncomfortably. "I wouldn't say it like that. But Samantha was quick, fast."

"Too fat to chase down someone then." Sawyer rubbed his chin, nodding slowly. "Maybe you're right."

"Hey," Campos retorted.

"You saying you're not?" Sawyer said, glancing back at the suspect.

"Imma sue you."

"So I've heard. Well, Dr. Beck, thank you for your insight. But as you're not a physician, I'll leave assessments about my suspect's victim-chasing abilities to the qualified, if that's all right with you."

Ilse blinked. "I wasn't trying to intrude. I just think it's pretty obvious he didn't—"

"Thanks, Doc. Really. Any other insights?"

She stared at him, clearly put off. He didn't tend to inflect his words with sarcasm, or any emotion really. But he was growing tired of this back and forth. He didn't like having a babysitter. Didn't much like therapists to begin with. And now, as he stared into those piggy little eyes of Mr. Campos, he could see violence lurking there.

Only one withdrawn complaint on the man's record. But Sawyer could smell *mean* from a mile away.

And Mr. Campos was oozing it. If he wasn't a killer, then it was only because he was too cowardly to follow through. Sawyer knew this sort of man through and through. Could see the violence in Campos's eyes. Could see it in the beading of the sweat on his jutting upper lip. Could see it hidden behind a veneer of stupid and belligerent.

This was a violent man, no doubt. The doc might have hidden behind her degrees and statistics and facts and observations, but at the end of the day, Sawyer was in the killer-catching business.

A spade was a spade.

A bastard was a bastard.

Dr. Beck was wrong about this man.

But what if she's right about Samantha?

Sawyer felt a flicker of… of something. Self-doubt? Not possible. Reconsideration, then? Perhaps. Mr. Campos was not a nice man, but that didn't mean he was involved in Samantha Wright's kidnapping. Still, there was a killer out there, on the highway. A killer trolling the roads and mountain passes. Two young women dead already. Now, Samantha missing. The same guy?

Maybe not Mr. Campos. But it wasn't like Sawyer had any other leads.

And so, that settled, he began to ease the door shut again. “Thank you, Dr. Beck. Have a good morning.”

“I—I really think—”

“Mhmm.”

Ilse sighed in frustration, and he could feel her staring at the side of his face.

CHAPTER FIFTEEN

Ilse refused to call a law enforcement agent a jackass. But she certainly might *think* it. She muttered beneath her breath as she pulled back into her driveway, piloting the Boat off the old forest road, toward the lake house. She put the vehicle in park and, still muttering darkly to herself, hopped out of the car. Now, the exhaustion was wearing not just on her mind, but also her emotions. Her eyes were heavy, hooded, and she felt them drooping every couple of steps, only for her to blink rapidly, opening them wide.

Ilse double-, then triple-checked the locks, before turning and moving toward the front of the house. The mist had cleared beneath the cresting sun, and the lake seemed more blue than gray. The trees surrounding the lake rustled, and pine needles trembled and plummeted, gathering on the ground or pattering to the surface of the water, where spreading ripples sent the detritus toward the embankment, wreathing the water in a halo of orange and green.

"Thank you, Dr. Beck," she muttered to herself, wrinkling her nose. "Thank you? Hmm. Thank you? Don't thank me. Not if you're going to..." She trailed off, marching up the steps and pausing next to her mailbox.

For a moment, she simply paused, rubbing the back of her head, and looking off across the lake. As she did, she heard rustling above, and glanced up, watching a squirrel dart from one branch to another. She heard a flutter—wings, perhaps? She watching as the squirrel pause, sniffing at something.

The brownish whiskers and swishing tail went still all of a sudden, frozen against the backdrop of dappled brown and green, stiff on the branch.

Ilse looked up, watching the squirrel, watching as it stared at something edged against the tree itself, braced between branch and bough.

A nest.

She stared at the nest, curious, watching the squirrel sniff at the gathering of twigs and leaves and old sticks. She swallowed, wondering if there were eggs in the nest. Wondering if perhaps the squirrel would try and steal one. Did they even do that?

It was hard to know, unless one paid attention, what sorts of predators existed in the wild. One always had to pay attention.

"Ridgway, Utah, forty-eight victims," she murmured softly to herself, barely voicing the words. Her eyes fixed on the squirrel, willing it to leave, willing it to dart away.

She heard the sound of fluttering wings again, from somewhere higher in the canopy, and this seemed to spook the whiskered woodland creature. The squirrel darted through the branches and disappeared, a trail of rattling leaves and shifting boughs the only clue to its presence.

The nest left undisturbed.

Not all nests fared so well.

A flash of memory, a jolt of fear. Ilse gasped as images swam across her vision. The struggling pigeon in her fingers. The fingers against her hand, rough and strong. The crunch. The tears slipping down Hilda Mueller's cheeks. The soft sobbing.

She hadn't been allowed to wash her hands. She'd been forced to take her *pet* to bed with her. To place it in her sleeping bag with her. Still sobbing, still crying.

"Don't cry, Hilda. Don't cry or you'll do it again tomorrow!"

She remembered the shadow over her. The screaming voice. The mismatched eyes, blue and brown, staring wild and furious down at her. Could remember the dusty basement, the eyes of her siblings, all of them pretending to be asleep, all of them pretending they couldn't hear.

She remembered trying to sleep. Unable to. Remembered the soft, pressing lump of the dead bird against her sleeping bag. Remembered the way it tickled her chin, the feathers splayed and stained as they were. Remembered her hands, unwashed, in pain. One of her own fingers sprained from the pressure of her father's grip.

Ilse blinked again, gasping, chest heaving, and she swallowed, clearing her throat where she stood on her porch.

For one moment, beneath the branches, staring off, she felt an urge to cry.

"Damn it," she murmured softly. "Damn it!" she insisted through gritted teeth. She stared across the old forest lanes weaving through the trees. Could hear the soft rustle of branches as the little squirrel above fled the nest. Running, running, running.

Victim or threat?

Ilse wasn't sure about herself. Wasn't sure what could have been… might have been.

She closed her eyes, focused once more, murmuring, "Lopez. Underage murders. Three hundred and fifty victims. Sexual sadist. Whereabouts unknown."

Focus... she thought to herself. *Focus.* Maybe Agent Sawyer had been right. Maybe she wasn't going to be much help with Samantha going missing. She shivered at the thought. Sometimes the squirrels escaped.

Other times, they didn't make it far.

Samantha had made it twenty years. Twenty whole years.

And then her tormentor had found her. Was it the same man? Was it the monster from her past?

Ilse rubbed at her hair, brushing it angrily past her ear. She paused next to the mailbox, freezing all of a sudden on the stoop of her doorstep.

A postcard in the box.

She knew what it was the moment her eyes landed. No junk mail this time. Just a single postcard. She swallowed once, staring, exhaling slowly. She didn't speak, couldn't think of anything to say.

For one wild moment she considered simply leaving it there, resting in the mailbox, untouched.

But her curiosity drew her fingers up and in. Her knuckles brushed against the rough, black-painted metal container. He fingers trembled, brushed the rough card stock. And then she pulled the postcard out, staring at it.

She looked at the message first.

Hilda Mueller.

Nothing else. Just the name. But this time, instead of a picture of the Black Forest, it was another picture. An image of a small, quaint little village in Germany. Freiburg. A village she remembered as a child. Barely, though. A faint, distant memory, somewhere in the basement of her collection of thoughts. Hidden, buried, forgotten. A memory of the small town where she'd once been allowed to visit. One of the only times she remembered being allowed outside the basement.

A field trip, he'd called it.

She frowned, trying to reach in, to snag the memory, to lift it to the surface and watch it play out.

But even as she did this, her knees almost gave out as a sudden, horrible surge of fear and terror flooded her at once. She felt the urge to run, to flee for cover. Felt a desire to scream, to cry.

She realized her eyes had gone blurry, and her fingers gripping the postcard were shaking.

The postcard fell from her fingertips now, fluttering to the ground, resting against the prickly doormat which simply read *Welcome.*

Not *Welcome Home.*

Just welcome.

Some people didn't deserve a home. Ilse knew she wasn't home.

Gasping, hyperventilating now, she stared at where the postcard had fallen. *Hilda Mueller.* A quaint, pretty picture of a small village.

And yet sheer terror flooded her being.

"Damn it," she murmured, softly. "Damn it!"

It couldn't be Mitchell. Could it? He wouldn't taunt her like this... Was she in danger? Should she call someone? Her instincts had failed last time. She hadn't taken Samantha seriously. And now... someone from Ilse's own past was back. Someone was hunting her. She could feel it.

Not Dr. Mitchell then. Someone else was sending the postcards. Someone who *knew.* But who? How was it possible? Just a sick joke?

She could only hope. Her fingers were still trembling, and she stared at the tattoo looping her wrist.

Take captive every thought...

But some thoughts were harder to master than others. Some thoughts had a mind of their own.

Her keys jangled, her fingers shaking so badly that it took five tries to find the keyhole. When she did, she paused for a moment, feeling a chill along her spine. "Wuornos. Six victims. Postpartum psychosis." But the rote memorization didn't help. The familiar words, the pattern, didn't soothe as it once had.

She was in danger. She could feel it. She should have acted sooner. Done something before—

A door slammed shut behind her.

She jolted, turning sharply. She heard footsteps approaching, and as she rounded to face the driveway, her fists bunched and she loosed a small scream.

CHAPTER SIXTEEN

"Ilse, are you okay?"

The scream faltered on her lips, transitioned to a soft little sob, and then a desperate gulp for air. Her exhaustion was now playing games with her. Her vision was still trembling, along with her fingers. The keys pressed against her ribs where she'd jolted back in fright, feeling the rigid metal jutting from the lock, pressed against her like a knife.

Or just like keys, she thought to herself. Not a knife. No threat. Just keys.

She watched as her old mentor left his Prius, looking quizzically up at her from beneath his bushy eyebrows. The length of his long, white beard brushed the top of his suit, and he maintained the perfect posture he always carried.

Ilse inhaled, exhaled, puffing her lips and blowing steadily. She glanced toward the postcard on the ground and surreptitiously stepped forward, her foot covering the card now while she made a big show of stretching.

She forced a smile, though it felt more like a grimace. "Don," she said, quickly, nodding in greeting. "Where's the bike?"

Dr. Mitchell glanced at his parked Prius and sighed. "Had my ride earlier this morning," he said. "Blew a tire, though. Have to patch it up before I can ride again, unfortunately." He glanced from Ilse, to her door, and then, like a spotlight, his eyes flicked to her foot on top of the postcard. Just as quickly, his gaze bounced up.

Ilse could feel her emotions a whirring mess. Pieces and fragments of pieces drifted loose and untethered in her thoughts, like divers severed from a ship, drifting in the murk away, away, away…

Sometimes a squirrel fled by choice, and other times by tragedy.

"What are you doing here?" she said, quickly, then wincing and realizing how hard her tone sounded. She coughed and adjusted. "I mean, it's nice to see you. But don't you have class in the morning?"

Dr. Mitchell smiled. "It's only seven, dear. Class doesn't start until nine." His prosthetic arm hung loose by his side. An open, vulnerable posture. His eyes fixed on her now, searching, concerned. "I just wanted to stop by," he said. "See how things were going with your new client."

Ilse blinked, swallowing. She could feel her foot stuck to the postcard as if rooted in cement. For one, brief moment she wanted to scream. To tell him everything, to let everything flood from her lips. Hell, he didn't even know her real name. Didn't know about Germany. Didn't even know her accent was practiced, learned.

No one knew. But no one could, could they? Some secrets were best left buried. Was she in danger, though? She didn't look at the postcard, shifting her weight a bit before saying, offhand, "You haven't been sending me postcards, have you?" She tried to keep her tone breezy, but Dr. Mitchell's eyes narrowed instantly. He stared at her, watching, searching, and she felt like she was a specimen being examined beneath a microscope.

At last, though, he shook his head. "No, dear. Should I have been? Are you all right, Ilse, you seem put out."

She tried to smile again, but the expression died before it even reached her lips.

She stepped down from her door now, taking the stairs and kicking back dust and pine needles for good measure, leaving the postcard where it had fallen. Dr. Mitchell was frowning. "Are you all right?" he said, softly, repeating the question, both concern and worry in his tone.

Ilse blinked as another memory surfaced. This one recollected, cataloged, held in a precious part of her thoughts. A memory of first meeting Dr. Mitchell. He'd caught her sneaking into his classes. She hadn't been a student at the time, not when they'd first met. He'd found it amusing that a teenager would want to take an advanced graduate class on Abnormal Psychology. Instead of kicking her out or reporting her, he'd invited her to his office. After one conversation, he seemed to have decided she was worth investing in.

Or perhaps that was too cynical a way to look at it.

Perhaps he'd simply been kind. He had kind eyes above his Santa Claus beard. Ilse often joked to her mentor that he looked like Kris Kringle on an Atkins diet. He'd often joke back, with equally good cheer, that if she didn't watch her lip, she'd end up with coal in her stocking.

Once, a few years ago, he'd even purchased her a whittled coal statue as a gift on Christmas, as a joke.

As the memories surfaced, swirling up, carrying on a current of fondness, warmth, quiet affection, she could feel some of the fear, the worry, the doubt, melting away like ice. She could feel the block in her stomach loosening a bit. Could feel the surfacing terror, pain dipping back beneath her subconscious again. At least for the moment.

Ilse hadn't realized she'd been breathing so shallowly until she took a long, shuddering breath, filling her lungs fully for the first time since exiting her car.

"I—something happened, Don," she said, her voice shaky. She could feel tears forming now.

Dr. Mitchell's own face creased, a painful expression. Pain for no other reason than she was hurting. "Oh, Ilse. Dear, dear, dear… What's the matter?"

He took her into an embrace first, hugging her quickly. He didn't expect an answer to start. The hug came before the answer. With Dr. Mitchell, it often did. She could feel his fuzzy beard against her cheek, his thin biker's body against her baggy sweatshirt. Her old mentor stepped back now, studying her, his eyes searching.

"Samantha," Ilse said, feeling her voice hoarse. She coughed delicately and glanced off. Her eyes traced the nearest tree, flicking up to where she'd spotted the small nest. She couldn't see it now.

She looked back at her old mentor, could feel the warmth emanating from him. Could still feel the warmth of his hug, like hot cocoa in mid-winter. She found her vision wasn't blurry anymore, and her fingers weren't trembling.

"Samantha went missing," she said, softly. "I heard her on the phone. She called me. It sounded like she was attacked."

Dr. Mitchell's eyes widened. Just as quickly, though, he hid the surprise, hid the shock. He knew he needed to be strong for her. How many times had Ilse done the same thing for the people who needed her help? Hiding her own emotions, burying them to tend to someone else's.

Dr. Mitchell shook his head, watching her carefully, gauging her reaction, gauging how he ought to respond for her sake. How he could best help her.

"I'm so, so sorry to hear that, Ilse. Samantha seemed like a nice lady. I shouldn't have sent her your way. I never would have if I'd known."

"It's not your fault. It isn't. Look, Don, I don't know what to do."

"Did you call the police?" he said, gently.

"Of course. Last night. They're already looking for suspects."

"So they haven't found her?" He winced, not finishing the thought. "That's a relief."

"Yeah… I just don't know what to do. What should I do?" *What should I do about the postcards? About my surfacing memories? What should I do about lying to you for fifteen years?* Ilse left the questions unvoiced. Not now. What good would it do now? Samantha was in trouble. Samantha mattered now. This wasn't about Ilse. It wasn't about Ilse's baggage. She needed to help her client. Samantha had come to her, and Ilse had failed her.

Dr. Mitchell was shaking his head sadly, his eyes carrying an ache on Ilse's behalf. He'd always had the ability to connect on a compassion level with his clients. Even the most difficult ones. Even the most dangerous ones. Ilse remembered seeing her old mentor hug a man on death row once, during a clinic at a prison. The man had dwarfed her instructor, but had broken down, bawling like a little babe in Dr. Mitchell's arms.

"I'm not sure there's much you can do, Becks," he said gently. He took her hand, patting it. "If you've told the police, I'm sure they're handling it, dear."

She nodded slowly. "I—I know," she said, clearing her throat. "But… I just feel like I need to… I don't know."

"There's nothing to do, Ilse. I know it's scary. But there isn't anything to do except keep your phone near in case you can help the investigators. Would you like to come with me to the university? You could sit in on one of the classes. Teach it if you like—might get your mind off things."

Ilse hesitated, gnawing her lip.

Smoothly, Dr. Mitchell said, "Or, if you like, I could call and cancel. Yes, I'll cancel. We can go for a drive, or get breakfast or something." He was fishing his phone out of his pocket already.

"No, don't cancel," Ilse said, quickly. "It's fine. Really." She exhaled. "It's just… just I feel like she's alive. I know she's still alive."

Dr. Mitchell nodded. But she could tell he didn't agree. He didn't say anything. He just nodded, showing he'd heard. He was a compassionate man, but not a bullshitter. He didn't participate in his clients' or students' or friends' delusions. He would listen, he would lend an ear, but he wouldn't encourage anything he thought was untrue.

Dr. Mitchell was a truthful man.

So how had Ilse ended up living such a double life? Where was the truth in her?

Still, it was different. At least, she had to think it was. She couldn't tell… not even her friend and mentor. Not anyone. Her fingers twitched once, and she massaged her pointer finger on her left hand briefly, feeling an old, cold ache as deep as bone.

"Ilse," Dr. Mitchell said, softly. "Don't play this out in your mind. Don't do that to yourself. It is out of your hands now."

"But it wasn't," she returned. "It wasn't! I could have helped, and I didn't."

"Let's go to breakfast. It's a small class anyway. Besides, Johnson owes me a substitute. I'm sure that—"

"I don't want breakfast, Don." Ilse paused, wincing at her tone. "Sorry. Sorry, I don't mean to bark. I just…"

"I understand, dear." Mitchell drew near, patting her on the shoulder and looking her firmly in the eyes, refusing to let go of her gaze. "But you can't undo what's been done. You can't go back to the start of things. All there is, is now."

Ilse could feel the force of his stare. Could feel the compassion in his gaze. But at the same time, she could feel her own heart hammering.

All there is, is now…

You can't go back to the start of things.

"Maybe not…" she murmured.

"Excuse me, dear?"

Ilse, though, slowly stepped away from her old mentor, moving back onto the lowest stair, then stepping onto the next. She snatched her keys from the door, her mind whirring.

"Ilse!" he said, slowly. "Ilse, please. Where are you going?"

She turned now, taking the stairs again, leaving the postcard behind her beneath dust and pine needles. Dr. Mitchell wasn't the only one who could suppress his own emotional reaction for the sake of someone else. Ilse had to as well. For Samantha. She needed to focus.

Perhaps she couldn't go back to the beginning. At least not in the way Dr. Mitchell meant it. She couldn't change what had been done.

But to remember? Not the two sessions she'd had. No. Not those.

Samantha had been certain. She'd been more than certain.

"Not paranoid…" Ilse murmured, moving past Dr. Mitchell now and hurrying toward the car. Her loose, baggy sweater and sweatpants felt like blankets swaddling her. The breeze from over the lake and the cresting sun through the trees felt like the kiss of something unseen.

"Ilse," Dr. Mitchell said, gentle but urgent. "Please, dear, leave it to the police."

She glanced back at her mentor, glimpsing a spurt of pain in his eyes. Something close to worry as he watched her.

She smiled now, and this time it wasn't forced. "I'm going to be fine, Don. I promise. I think you're right, though. The clue is at the beginning. Where it all started."

"I—I don't know—Ilse, that's not what I meant. Please. Let's get breakfast, dear!"

But Ilse gave a faint little shake of her head. She paused, though, took two skipping steps back, and gave Dr. Mitchell a quick hug, kissing him on the cheek and patting his shoulder. Then, nodding even more determinedly to herself, feeling her lips itch from her old mentor's whiskers, she hurried back to her waiting vehicle.

She climbed into the Boat as Dr. Mitchell watched her. He no longer spoke, just sighing and waiting. He would be there for her. He was always there for her. But he never intruded. He never manipulated.

Besides, even if he had, Ilse wasn't willing to be controlled. Not again. Not ever.

She turned the keys and began to edge out of the driveway in the Boat. Past the Prius. She waved a quick goodbye to her old mentor and then floored the gas, kicking up dust and pine needles as she raced back to the police station.

Back to the beginning…

It was the only thing left.

CHAPTER SEVENTEEN

Sawyer sighed as he closed the interrogation room door behind him with a soft *click*. His fist bunched at his side, but at least he hadn't let it loose. A mild improvement. He was on thin ice as it was. After what had happened back in Oakland, punching a suspect would be the last straw.

Still, Mr. Campos hadn't made it easy. If anyone deserved a good walloping, it was that man.

Not that he'd admitted to anything. And not that Sawyer was convinced he was involved in this kidnapping. But that was a vicious man if ever he'd seen one. Not just the assault charge. But something about that sickly look in the man's eyes. Something deep as soul.

Sawyer paused, crossing himself and offering a little prayer up. He didn't consider himself a religious man. Though others might. Sometimes he simply enjoyed how the gesture offended some. Anything to raise the hackles. But other times, he found it soothing, comforting and true. He found strength hidden there too, in surprising ways.

Maybe the doc would have a thought or two about it.

Not that he'd ever speak on it with her.

Even then, as he turned back toward the break room, feeling a flicker of frustration at the sealed interrogation room door and the equally sealed lips of his suspect, he blinked in surprise at the woman stalking toward him across the hall from the sliding glass doors.

Sawyer paused, pulling up and coming to a standstill as Dr. Ilse Beck strode toward him. She still wore the oversized, unflattering baggy sweater and sweatpants, as if she didn't want to attract the least bit of attention. She didn't wear makeup, though she was pretty in an understated way. Now, though, she was frowning, and one hand brushed nervously at her hair over her right ear.

He hadn't spotted it at first, but as she neared, beneath the light above, he noticed the thin trail of a scar along her chin, disappearing behind her low-hanging hair.

He sighed and waited, watching as she drew near.

"Agent Sawyer," she said in greeting, her voice flustered, her movements hurried and urgent.

"Mhmm?"

"Get anywhere with the suspect? I suppose you probably aren't allowed to tell me. But I just wanted to say I think—"

"Lawyered up. How can I help you, Doc?"

"I was thinking," she said, quietly. "Remembering a conversation I had with my client, with Samantha. Not one of our sessions. It didn't come to mind right away. It was on the phone. She was scared."

"Hmm?"

"Hmm indeed. Yes. Look, I know it's a long shot. But I remember now; but Samantha was sure she was being re-targeted by an old threat. By the man who'd kidnapped her when she was only a child. Nearly twenty years ago."

He watched her, nodding once for her to continue.

She sighed in mild frustration, but pressed on regardless. "Look, I remember something she said. That little window I mentioned. The one she said she would watch the red truck from? She also saw something else. She described the place where she was abused. Where she barely escaped."

His eyebrows flicked up. "Oh? Where?"

"An abandoned shack on an old farm. It's possible, if it's the same attacker, that he took her there. Somehow, he found her again, after all these years…" Ilse paused, swallowing, and for a moment, her expression flickered with something else… Fear? Guilt?

Sawyer stared, for the first time wondering if perhaps double-checking Dr. Beck's own alibi might be worth a shot. She was hiding something. Everyone did. But whatever she was hiding hung heavy on her, like wet tissue. He could see it in her posture, in her eyes, in the way she spoke. The eagerness she had to *help.* Most people helped out of a sense of obligation. Or penance. Or absolution.

Guilty people helped just as often as compassionate ones. And the two were rarely exclusive.

Sawyer watched her for a moment. Then said, "You didn't have anything to do with this, did you?"

She blinked, staring. For a moment, her features froze. And then her eyes flashed with anger. Her jaw set in a defiant way. He watched her hands, though. Expressions were easy for practiced liars. Features could be arranged. But hands?

Hands weren't for feeling, or expressing.

Hands were for action.

And Ilse's remained flat, glued to her thighs. They didn't bunch, they didn't posture for violence. If anything, she froze—straight fear.

He watched her a second longer, watched the anger sparking in her eyes, her hands flat to her thighs. Not a violent woman, then. But a secretive one. A liar? Maybe. Probably.

A trustworthy liar?

Maybe. Probably.

"No," she was saying, her voice like iron. "I didn't have anything to do with this!"

"You look angry and guilty," he said, completely unaffected by the flash of passion in her tone. "You're helping too much. More than normal. Makes me suspect you."

She crossed her arms. "You accused me of kidnapping my own client. Of course I'm angry."

"See, there too. Didn't address the guilt part. Didn't address the helping too much part. Like I said, I suspect you. Don't know of what. Least not yet."

"More instincts?" she said. "Do you *feel* it in your gut? How's that worked so far?" She waved a hand toward the sealed interrogation room door. "Can't help but notice, *Tom*, you don't have too many cops lining up to give you a hand here. Some of them seemed to treat you like you have the plague. Work trouble, hmm? Get into with some of the locals?" She paused, frowned, but then shook her head. "Or maybe a boss? Did you do something to piss off someone at the FBI? Is that why you've been isolated up and out of the way here?"

Sawyer blinked in surprise. Instead of reacting in anger at the fishing, he nodded, mildly impressed. "Not bad," he said. "All right. Maybe I believe you. Say again; what are we looking for?"

Ilse gave a little shake of her head as if to reorient herself, but then, clearly and crisply, she said, "An old abandoned shack on an old farm. And…" She paused, one hand reaching out for a moment as if miming opening a door. Her eyes flickered and then she nodded quickly. "An old weather vane in the shape of a rooster. Bent and rusted, she said."

"She? Ms. Wright?"

"She prefers Sam."

Sawyer shrugged. "Right. Not much to go on, Doc."

"Got anything else? Besides me and Mr. Campos, I mean?" Her words fell heavy and firm.

Agent Sawyer scratched his chin, but then turned, nodding and giving a little flick of his finger, gesturing she should follow. He heard her sigh in frustration behind him, but at least, by the sound of her footsteps, she'd fallen into line.

"Better than nothing," he said over his shoulder. He moved past the sergeant's desk and toward one of the office spaces beyond the interrogation room. A few eyes darted up and over at the odd pairing of the therapist in sweats and the FBI agent in flannel and a baseball cap, but then Sawyer waved toward the sergeant with the pixie cut.

"Faber," he said.

The sergeant glanced over her computer monitor, one hand gripping a steaming mug. She frowned. "Tom?" she said. She glanced toward the window as if double-checking the time of day, and then shook her head. "Christ, Tom, did you sleep at all last night?"

"Hmm. Look, I need some help from you guys."

"It's barely eight," she muttered. "Gonna be mostly half-assed help."

"Pair the asses," Sawyer said. "I need some of your folk to check maps and aerial photography."

"Where?"

"Surrounding area."

"*How* surrounding, Tom?"

Agent Sawyer scratched his chin, glancing out the window himself for a moment, before clearing his throat. "Twenty-, thirty-mile radius."

Faber let out a long, intentional sigh. She tilted her head back and stared at the popcorn ceiling tiles. "You're joking."

"'Fraid not."

"All right… And what should I tell them we're looking for?"

Sawyer jutted a thumb toward Dr. Beck in answer. The dark-haired woman stepped forward, nodding politely in greeting. Faber just raised an eyebrow, taking a long, loud sip off coffee.

"Hello, I'm Ilse."

"Sergeant Faber. Nice to meet you. You're the one who called in the missing person last night, yes?"

Ilse nodded quickly. "Yes, I am. She's my client."

"Client?"

"I'm a therapist."

Sergeant Faber's eyes widened in delight. "Oh, really? What are your rates? I've been looking for a new—"

Sawyer cleared his throat, and Faber shot him a nasty look. She sighed, amending her expression and returning her attention to Ilse. She paused for a moment, glancing toward the office space, the computers, then back at Tom. "Is she… she technically supposed to be back here?" Faber said, tilting her eyebrows significantly. She flashed an apologetic look toward Ilse, but returned her severe look to Sawyer.

Tom shrugged. Chasing down serial killers out in the field was one thing, but desk work? As far as he saw it, anyone with a pair of eyes and an attention span could help with desk work. "She's a consultant."

"Really? Because normally I'm the one who handles consultant paperwork. And I don't remember—"

"She is," Tom cut the sergeant off. "Forget the paperwork. Look, like you said—it's morning. You saying your crew won't appreciate another pair of eyes?"

Faber paused for a moment, but then sighed and waved a hand. "Have it your way. You can use that computer, Doctor—though I'm going to be supervising. *Closely.*"

"Got it," Ilse said, nodding.

Sawyer just shrugged.

Faber returned her attention to Ilse. "So what should I note as landmarks? If we're going to search for a needle in a haystack, it would be nice to at least have as many magnets as possible."

"Ah, yes," said the doc, "I see. Well, there should be an old, abandoned farm, with a big barn. It's probably weather worn and dilapidated at this point. Though it's possible it was renovated."

"All right, old abandoned farm. Big barn. Anything else?"

"Yes, actually. We're looking especially for a small, run-down shack on the property. The shack should have a bent and rusted weather vane on top. In the shape of a rooster."

"A rooster weather vane. Pretty common accessory."

"On the shack, though. Not the barn."

Sergeant Faber sighed, but did her best to keep chipper, bobbing her head after another sip of coffee. "All right, I can probably get Dennings and Adler on it. Maybe Vick."

"Good." Sawyer began to turn. "Let me know if you find any—"

"Fat chance!" Faber interrupted. "You better believe you're helping. Both of you. Morning shift is skeleton. Those two computers. Have at it."

Faber pointed to two seats within eye-line of her own desk. At the same time, as she kept a commanding finger jutting toward the spare desks, she was also gesturing toward the back of the office space, raising her voice and calling, "Dennings, Adler. Grab Vick! Nah—drop it. Print it after. I got something else for you."

Sawyer heard a chorus of groans from the back of the room, but he was too busy moving over toward the indicated computers himself. Desk work.

He wrinkled his nose in disgust. Yuck.

Still, sometimes desk work led to field work. First veggies, then dessert.

He nodded to himself, stretching his long, lanky form out in the office chair and watching sidelong as Dr. Beck stationed herself at one of the computers next to him marked for guests. It looked, for a moment, like she was having difficulty figuring out how to turn it on. They waited for Sergeant Faber to log them in, where she could keep an eye on them, and then watched as three other bleary-eyed, coffee-sipping morning shift cops moved over with lead feet and deep scowls.

The dream team.

Sawyer snorted, already cycling to the web browser while Faber began to break down the instructions for the rest of the officers. Needle in a haystack indeed.

Still, there was a young woman out there. And while Sawyer never made things personal, he knew time was running out. *Tick, tick.* Someone had Ms. Wright in their hands. Someone up to no good.

If they didn't hurry, it would all be too late.

***

The sun was hidden again behind the gloomy, overcast skies through the window. The three police officers gathered around Faber's desk, slapping printed pages next to her computer. Faber smiled sweetly up at each of them. "Thank you very much," she said, teasing their gloomy countenances with her chipper tone.

Sawyer also stood by the desk, staring at his meager pile of printed photos. Dr. Beck, next to him, had a smaller stack than his.

The overcast skies outside competed with the fluorescent lights inside the precinct. The afternoon stretched, threatening evening soon enough. Sawyer could feel a crick in his back and his eyes ached from staring at the screen so long. Exhaustion pulsed through him, but he reached into his pocket, pulling out a small, white pill—caffeine—and popped it into his mouth, swallowing without water. He glanced over to Dr. Beck, who looked like a ghost. Her face pale, her eyes drooping. Sleep was in short supply all around, it seemed.

"Well," Faber said, stacking the printed pictures and handing them to Sawyer. "There we have it. Anything else I can do for you, your highness?"

The three other officers were moving, heading back to their desks. Before they'd gotten far, though, Sawyer cleared his throat. "Not so fast," he muttered. "Need feet on the pavement."

One of the officers shot an irritated look at the lanky agent. "FBI has its own people, doesn't it?" the man snapped.

But Faber clucked her tongue and held up a hand. "Hang on, Vick," she murmured. "We're supposed to help our dear friend from the Bureau in any way we can. Right? Or was the captain unclear?"

The man named Vick muttered darkly and crossed his arms over his chest. "Maybe I should punch my boss. Get special treatment that way myself," he muttered.

Sawyer ignored the jibe, but he could feel Dr. Beck's eyes flick toward him, searching and curious.

He tapped a finger on the printed aerial photos from the GPS maps they'd combed. He looked at Ilse. "Well," he said. "Which ones?"

Ilse hesitated, but then nodded to herself as if summoning courage, stepped forward, and delicately took the stack of photos from Sergeant Faber. Slowly, the doc sifted through the photos. She studied one at a time before placing them in two separate piles.

"No weather vane," she murmured, placing one of the photos to one side. "Barn wouldn't be visible from the shack," she continued, softly, placing another one in the same discard pile. "This one though… maybe. Maybe…"

Everyone waited, watching the civilian sort through the pictures. Sawyer frowned as she did, wondering if perhaps he was putting too much time and energy behind the instincts of a therapist of all things. He'd never call her a duck to her face, but eventually, in his estimation, everyone in her field went quack.

Still, she'd managed to peg him on a thing or two. A broken clock was right at least a couple times a day.

So he waited quietly, watching as she sorted the photos. At last, she tapped them. "Those," she said, pointing to the pile on the right. "Those are our best bets."

Faber glanced at Sawyer, waiting for his confirmation.

"Mhmm," he said.

"Right," Faber said, grabbing the newly indicated pile. Before she could, though, Dr. Beck snatched the top photo. "This one is ours," she said, quickly.

Everyone gave her a look. "Ours?" Faber asked.

Beck glanced at Sawyer. "Yeah. I'm coming with. If I'm right, then I got us this far," she added, quickly.

"And if you're wrong," Faber murmured, "you just wasted forty man hours." She sighed, though, looking at Sawyer again. "You're the fed. This is your rodeo. You want the doc to pair up?"

"Why that one?" Sawyer asked, nodding at the photo she'd picked off the stack.

Ilse's eyes narrowed. She didn't blink. "I'll tell you on the way."

"Right. She's with me," Sawyer said, shrugging at Faber, who smirked.

"Fine," Faber said. "The rest of you grab a photo. Head to the address. Call backup if you see anything *untoward.* You know what that word means, Vick?"

The man snorted. "Untowards your face, Faber."

The pixie-cut sergeant snorted. "Good one. Right, well, grab a photo. Head off. Guess the Bureau's taking cues from civies now."

Sawyer tapped Ilse on the arm. Before he could indicate she follow, though, she stepped past him and quickly moved ahead. Then, without looking back, she beckoned him with a crook of her finger. He blinked after her for a moment as she strode away, the photo clutched in one hand.

Despite himself, a small smile crept across his lips. He hid it in a cough, though, and then followed Dr. Beck out of the precinct.

Was she right after all? What were the odds? Had she remembered Samantha Wright's words correctly? Had Ms. Wright remembered the past correctly?

Somewhere out there, Samantha's time was running out. They didn't have another lead. Maybe there was a chance… a chance of a chance. Maybe, just maybe, they had a chance at finding this old abductor's address. Active for twenty years…

Sawyer shivered, frowning as he did. He wouldn't make it personal. Couldn't allow it. But even for him, the thought made his skin crawl.

He could only hope Dr. Beck was right. Otherwise, things were looking grim for Samantha Wright.

CHAPTER EIGHTEEN

The gloomy, overcast weather marked the horizon as Ilse watched Agent Sawyer drive through the narrow roads south of the city. At least this time, he'd allowed her a seat up front, though he'd seemed reluctant to do so.

Ilse's eyes kept darting from the printed photo in her hand to the road ahead of them. The GPS from Agent Sawyer's phone kept chirping. His eyes were fixed on the road. As they traversed beneath gray skies, Agent Sawyer murmured, "Tell me again why we can't use your phone's GPS?"

This was the first he'd spoken to her in the nearly twenty-minute drive south from the station. She cleared her throat delicately, glancing toward the lanky form of the BAU agent. "I have a dumb phone," she murmured. "It doesn't have GPS." She pulled out her old flip phone to show it to him.

He glanced over, then returned his attention back to the road. A few moments passed, but then, to her surprise, he spoke again. "You're not a drug dealer, are you?"

It took her a second to realize he was joking. "Umm, no. I just like the phone. Not a big fan of technology. I have a wood-burning stove back home, actually." She wasn't sure why she'd volunteered this last part. But for some reason it seemed to prompt a ghost of a smile on Agent Sawyer's normally dour lips.

"I see," he said.

They drifted off into silence again, and Ilse did her best not to shoot glances in his direction. A strange case study, Agent Tom Sawyer. Named, it seemed, after a character from a novel. A novel written by an author who'd hidden his name. Samuel Clemens to Mark Twain.

Not too unlike Hilda Mueller to Ilse Beck.

Maybe the two of them had something in common after all. However small though it was.

"There we are," Sawyer murmured, nodding through the windshield to an old, dead field a second before the GPS chirped, *Arriving at destination on your left.*

Sawyer piloted the vehicle smoothly onto the dirt road, past the broken, dusty field. The car jolted and bumped. A branch had fallen, forcing Sawyer to veer off into the dirt and then back onto the road, kicking up a cloud of dust which wafted to meet the gray, glaring skies.

In the distance, through the dust and past the low-hanging, arching boughs, withered much in the same way as the surrounding fields, a creepy scene confronted them.

A vacant, abandoned farm. The fields were tell-tale, but the rusted, overgrown tractor and combine added to the desolate scene. Old farm equipment piled against the side of a large, red barn. Ilse glanced at the photograph in her hand, then tracing a finger, she pointed off behind an overgrown patch of forest.

"The old shack should be back there," she murmured in a faint voice, feeling a chill rise along her spine.

The trees seemed larger, darker than they had from the main road. Now, as they trundled along toward the old barn, and the weathered farmhouse on the flat land, facing the dead field and the abandoned farm apparatus, Ilse could feel her mind flitting, sifting through the basement of her memories. Her fingers gripped each other, hard, and she swallowed, shivering against the rising thoughts.

Agent Sawyer glanced at her. "You okay?" he said, quietly, his voice oddly gentle and gruff at the same time.

"Fine," she murmured. "The shack should be just past there."

No movement from the farmhouse. A flutter of birds who'd hidden out behind the rusted tractor scattered toward the sky as they drew nearer. A crackling, cracking sound arose from old sticks and dried boughs across the road as the sedan moved closer to their target.

Suddenly, a loud *bang*. Then the car jolted to the left.

Ilse yelped, but Sawyer cursed, slamming a hand to the top of the wheel and immediately bringing the car to the side of the road and throwing on the brake.

"What was that?" Ilse demanded, her heart pounding as she glanced around, her eyes on the farmhouse, tracing to the barn, then back to the very edge of a weathered, but hidden building behind the overgrowth.

"Flat tire," Sawyer replied, kicking open his door and sliding his lanky legs out onto the dusty road. "Wait inside."

Ilse paused, then huffed. "Hang on," she said, firmly, "I'm not staying here."

Sawyer looked through the window at her. "You're not coming with. Stay in the car."

"Oh? And what if the killer sneaks up on me while you're off searching the farm?"

Sawyer paused for a moment, tongue in his cheek, but then sighed, gesturing at her.

Ilse wasn't sure if she'd *wanted* to win this particular battle. Locked behind the car's doors seemed a safer location than anywhere on the farm. But she had to remind herself why she was here. *Who* she was here for. She pushed out of the vehicle, her eyes on the old, creepy fields, feeling suddenly very alone and isolated. She stepped delicately out onto the dirt road, exhaustion weighing heavily on every movement. She circled the front of the unmarked sedan and approached where Sawyer was on one knee, grumbling and poking with a pale finger at the front left wheel.

"What happened?" Ilse said.

"Nail," he replied. He tapped a finger on a jutting metal spike in the tire. Already, the thing was deflated beyond use. "Damn it," he growled, slapping a hand against the hood of the car. He turned, glancing along the trail, and then his frown deepened further.

"What is it?" Ilse said, reading his expression.

Instead of answering, he began to move carefully toward a portion of the road they'd passed. He pulled up short, staring down. One of his hands twitched toward the holster on his belt.

"Agent Sawyer?" she pressed, peering in closer. Ilse looked past Sawyer's form, his looming shadow cast as a dark streak against the gray road. There, dull and scattered across the ground, she spotted more nails, as well as screws and small jutting pieces of metal.

They'd been left in a line across the dirt road.

A chill crept up Ilse's spine. "Oh," she said, softly. "Think—think someone's here?" she added, dropping her voice to a whisper.

The line of metal fragments, though only an inch off the ground at the highest point, seemed a veritable battlement, warning off intrusion.

"Someone doesn't want visitors," Sawyer murmured, unbuttoning his holster and resting his thumb on his gun. "Interesting." He looked at her. "Stay near me and *behind* me. Or, if you'd rather…"

"I'm not waiting in the car."

He massaged the bridge of his nose, but then shrugged. "Stay close. Stay careful." He breathed slowly, calming. If anything, he seemed more relaxed once he'd seen the trail of nails and screws. An accident, it seemed, would have irritated him. A booby trap, though? Almost as if he relished it.

Ilse followed as he began to stride away from the car, circling the undergrowth in the direction she'd originally indicated. "This way, hmm?" he mouthed softly. "How about we take a little look... Remember, don't go off on your own, Doc."

The creepy scene of dead fields, vacant barn, rusted tractor, and old farm equipment beneath the overcast skies only further seemed to prod shivers up Ilse's back. Her fingers clutched the piece of paper with the printed aerial photograph as she followed Sawyer, and she glanced at it again. There she spotted the fields. There was the barn. And there... behind the overgrowth...

The abandoned shack with what, from the image, had looked like a twisted and dented weather vane. It had been hard to make out in the picture...

But of all the pictures it had looked the closest to an old rooster.

Now, as she followed Sawyer along the path, cautiously circling the overgrowth, she partly wished she'd been wrong. Hoping, now, in at least a portion of her psyche, that they were at the wrong farm...

As they rounded the path, the shack came into view.

Worn boards with rusted nails and a large crossing beam shut off the front door. Slits in the walls and a weathered portion of a caved in roof gave little in the way of protection from the elements. Most eye-catching to Ilse, though, was the weather vane on the very top of the crumbling roof.

Rusted, bent...

And shaped like an old rooster.

"Sawyer," she said, sharply, staring at the broken-down bird.

"I see it," he said, his eyes fixed on the front entrance itself. "Stay behind me," he added, quietly.

His shadow stretched behind him, passing over Ilse as he slowly pulled his firearm from its holster. Ilse's heart hammered as she stared at the gun as it reached Sawyer's fingers. She'd never been particularly comfortable around guns. She'd never owned one. Especially given the sorts of clients she had at her house. One of them might accidentally have stumbled on the thing.

She shivered, staring as Sawyer stalked toward the door of the abandoned shack.

"Hello?" he called out, his voice low and hoarse. "Anyone in there?"

Something banged behind them, and Ilse whirled sharply around. It took her a second to realize the screen door of the old farmhouse had been caught by the wind and sent slamming into the rail of the porch.

She huffed, unsure whether to follow Sawyer or stay put on the road.

After a second, she decided it was far worse to be on her own and so, tentatively, keeping her distance, she followed the agent closer to the door of the abandoned shack.

"FBI!" he called, his voice louder now. "Is anyone in there?"

No answer, save the wind, and another *bang* of the screen door. Ilse felt like her heart nearly jumped out of her chest, and she gritted her teeth.

Sawyer kept his gun in one hand, but his other probed out, long fingers pressing against the wooden beam across the front of the door. With a soft grunt, he lifted it, dust dislodging and sent scattering.

Not *so* much dust, though. Not as much as there should have been.

"Hello?" he said, softly, allowing the wooden beam to lodge against the edge of the door. Then, gun in one hand, raised, he gripped the handle to the shack and yanked it open without so much as a gasp of breath.

For a moment, he stood facing the darkness, Ilse peering over his shoulder. His breathing came soft, while Ilse gasped in ragged puffs. She missed a warm cup of tea, sitting on her couch, staring out at the lake and talking with her clients.

This was an entirely different sort of thing. She knew immediately she didn't like it. Not at all.

But Sawyer didn't seem bothered by the dark, shadowy shack. He stepped in without hesitating, his voice still clearing the dust and the way before him. "Hello?" he called, louder now. "FBI. We're here to help!"

Someone had scattered those nails. Someone hadn't wanted visitors. The weather vane… a crooked, bent rooster.

Ilse felt like a small, frightened girl again, trapped in a basement. She felt helpless, defenseless, protected only by a shadow and his gun. She frowned at this, feeling something stir in her chest. Memories played in her mind, but she pushed them aside, focusing on her own steady breathing.

She was no child anymore. No child at all. Then, if only to force herself to do something besides quake in her shoes, she called out, softly, "Samantha? Are you here?"

Both of them went quiet, just within the shack. No response. No sound. Not even the wind paid them mind this time.

The shack was empty. A small little loft pressed into the back of the cramped space. Strands of hay littered the loft, but a gaping hole in the floor of it gave a view of the weather-worn ceiling above. Around them, the walls were old, molding and in ill repair.

A few old, rusted barrels were scattered against one side of the shack. And a rider mower, red paint now turned orange and mealy, sat abandoned in the darkest corner.

A sudden beam of light shone from Sawyer, as he raised his phone and wielded it around the small area. The light illuminated the loft first, confirming it was empty. It moved to the barrels, and Sawyer stepped in.

For one horrible moment, as he peered into a barrel, Ilse expected the worst. But Sawyer moved on, glancing at her. "Empty," he murmured. He shone the light behind the rusted rider mower in the darkest portion of the shack.

No movement. Nothing. Just cobwebs and dust and neglect.

With a soft, almost disappointed sigh, Sawyer lowered his weapon, reholstering it and pulling out his radio. "Faber," he said, pressing the speaker. "Hear me?"

A crackling voice Ilse couldn't make out replied.

"Any of you find anything?" Sawyer said. "The south farm's a—" He stopped, frowning.

Another crackling response came over the speaker, and Sawyer said, softly, "Hang on." His eyes narrowed, fixated on the small little rider mower in the back of the shack.

The sound of the crackling radio drifted off into the background as Sawyer began to move slowly forward. "No windows…" he murmured.

"What was that?" Ilse asked.

Sawyer glanced at her. The tall, lanky man almost looked like a scarecrow in his flannel and jeans standing amidst scattered hay and dust.

"No windows," he repeated, a bit more loudly this time. "Your client said she'd watch an old red truck *through* a window. She said she was kept in the shack."

Ilse blinked, momentarily impressed at the agent's memory. "So we're at the wrong place."

Sawyer clicked off the radio and it went eerily silent. "Or there's a basement. And the window has been blocked off."

"Basement?"

But Sawyer was already approaching the old rider mower. He frowned at it for a moment, but then, avoiding as many cobwebs as possible—while Ilse shivered, trying not to think of all the creepy crawlies with fangs likely hidden around—he pushed against the upraised, plastic seat. The grimy, dusty surface pressed against his fingers.

Sawyer grunted in exertion, but at the same time, the mower began to move. All four of its wheels were clearly flat. It took a second, as he shoved, and Ilse moved over to help. But before she reached him, the mower lifted over two wooden blocks, and then trundled forward, carried by its own momentum, past Ilse, and bumping gently against the door.

"Thing looks like it's been in here for years," Ilse murmured, staring at the rider mower.

"Yes," Sawyer said, softly, eyes narrowed shrewdly. "Look at the wheels, though."

Ilse did, and then murmured, "No dust."

He nodded. "Flat, everything else caked in grime. But no dust on top of the wheels. Means it's been moved."

Now, Sawyer clicked his flashlight back on, shining it toward the floor.

Ilse felt her heart jolt. Sawyer whistled softly, muttering up a quiet prayer. He crossed himself with his free hand.

A hatch centered the floorboards.

CHAPTER NINETEEN

Ilse stared at the hatch, her heart hammering.

"Doc, you should get back to the car," Sawyer said, softly, his hand glued to his holster.

"No," she said quickly. "That's just as dangerous. Better I'm here with you. Besides," she swallowed, her voice laden, "she's *my* client."

Sawyer gave her a long look, but then shrugged. He moved toward the hatch, and Ilse followed a second later, swallowing her fear.

Ilse and Sawyer pulled the hatch together, both of them grunting in exertion. No dust, though—the hinges didn't even creak. It had been used recently, then.

Ilse felt another shiver down her spine, breathing heavily as she settled the hatch against the floor and found herself staring at a set of concrete steps leading down into darkness. Sawyer's flashlight illuminated the steps.

"Is that blood?" Ilse said, suddenly, pointing.

"Grease," Sawyer replied. "From the mower." He gave her a long look. "You okay?"

"Fine." Though she wished her voice hadn't sounded so high-pitched. It seemed to convince Sawyer, though, and he stepped onto the top step of the basement. Then the next, his gun back in his hand. His boot scraped the grease stain. She stared at where it smeared; it certainly looked even more like blood now.

For a moment, she stood in the old, abandoned shack alone, beneath the dusty, weathered walls and roof, inhaling the scent of moldy straw and grime. She stared at the basement, heart hammering, closing her eyes for a second.

Her lips buzzed, memories flitting to the surface.

She hated basements. Her house by the lake certainly didn't have one. That fact alone had ruled out any possibility of living in the Midwest. She stared at the concrete steps, at the streaked stain of grease… or blood.

Stared toward the darkness where Sawyer had vanished, the movement and flicker of his flashlight casting strange shadows behind him against the geometric slab steps.

Did she really want to venture into the basement? If she didn't, could she forgive herself? What if Samantha was down there? What if she was hurt?

Ilse tried to step forward. She truly tried. But her feet felt rooted to the spot. Her hands were clammy, opening and closing on either side. She gripped the hem of her baggy sweater, panting softly, trying to force herself to move.

But she stood rooted, motionless.

"Come here, Hilda!"

"No…." she murmured. "No, I won't…"

"I won't hurt you…"

"Yes," she said, shakily, staring at the gaping entrance to the dark basement. "Yes, you will."

"Come here, Hilda!"

Her fingers probed up to her maimed ear, tracing the scar on the right side of her face. She couldn't bring herself to move. She couldn't—

"Doc, get down here!" Sawyer's voice suddenly shouted, alarmed.

Ilse's pulse raced. The single note of fear in Sawyer's voice, a note she hadn't heard from the lanky agent until that moment, jolted her into motion. It was as if her foot was released from some unseen grip. Despite herself, despite every synapse in her brain screaming against the movement, she stumbled forward, *into* the basement, down the slab steps, stepping over the slab with the grease stain.

The basement was small, cramped…

And it smelled like a meat locker.

The odor alone nearly sent Ilse stumbling back, gagging on the air. She pulled her sweater over her nose, breathing shallowly, but even then, her eyes watered and ached. With shallow, puffing breaths, she located the beam of flashlight from Sawyer's phone. He was standing in the far corner of basement, directly beneath where the loft was situated in the room above.

His flashlight illuminated something in the dark, pressed against the wall. Was that a raccoon? No—bigger. Was that…

Ilse felt her heart pound as she stumbled forward, drawn like a moth to flame, moving toward Sawyer, his gun and his flashlight.

"What is it?" she called.

"Doc, you need to tell me if this one's breathing." He kept one hand on his flashlight, the other on his weapon, seemingly loath, in that moment, to lower either. His eyes whirled about, as if expecting some threat to burst from the ceiling at any second.

Ilse's pulse quickened, and as she drew near, her gaze finally settled in the dark and dust. Not a raccoon at all, but a torso, attached to legs beneath a fallen log beam.

A body.

Ilse nearly screamed, holding a hand against the sweater pressed over her lips. She began to dry heave, sobbing into her sweater.

"Doc, please. Alive?" Already, Sawyer was pressing his radio, and as she moved in, she heard him speaking crisply and clearly over the speaker, contacting the police back at the precinct.

For her part, a small little portion of her wanted to say something like, "I'm not that type of doctor." But passing the buck now wasn't an option. No one else was there.

She leaned in with trembling fingers, pressing them against the neck of the victim, feeling for a pulse. A man. Not Samantha. Someone she didn't recognize.

No pulse at all. Cold skin. The smell alone should have been notice enough.

She reeled back, wiping her fingers angrily off on her pants, and then feeling the urge to burn her sweats. "Dead," she said, suddenly. She reeled back, but then tripped with a shout, yelling as she landed against something soft, like a pillow.

Something that also smelled.

Ilse scrambled to her feet, whirling, and this time she screamed; a full-throated, horrified sound. Sawyer's light wheeled around and illuminated the horrible scene. Rats crawling, creeping, slinking. They scattered all at once, leaving behind the corpses they'd been nibbling on.

Five other bodies, as far as Ilse could tell. Bodies arranged strangely. Despite the panic, the horror, the terror, another part of Ilse realized someone had gone to great lengths to arrange the bodies against the ground in a pattern.

It looked like a smiley face. Two corpses for eyes, three for a leering grin. All of them motionless, cold… *dead.*

Dead. Dead. Dead.

"Sawyer!" Ilse screamed. "Sawyer!"

"I see them," he said, quickly. "I see. Same as the first?"

"You can check for a pulse just as well," she snapped back, her temper flaring, prompted by smoldering fear turned to actual terror.

Sawyer swallowed once, then slowly holstered his weapon, though

Ilse wished he wouldn't. The flashlight shuddered and swung as he approached the bodies. One at a time, he bent down, checking wrists and throats.

After each body, he gave a faint little shake of his head. His radio crackled and he gave a quiet response Ilse didn't even catch, standing in that horrible, horrible basement. She spotted the window vaguely, doing her best to look anywhere but in the direction of the bodies. The window, indeed, had been covered up. Not with boards, though, but rather with a curtain. For a moment, Ilse wondered if there might have been another entrance into the basement, through that window. By the direction it faced, it would have led out of the side of the shack, toward the woods. Enough to give a glimpse of any approaching truck, but also directed away from the main road, save the portion nearest the farmhouse.

"Sawyer," Ilse said, shakily. "Sawyer, I think I'm going to be sick."

The agent was on his knee next to the final body, arranged in the left corner of the mouth. And then he stiffened. A soft, gasping sound echoed through the room. Then a weak, tired little voice. "Help me… Help me, please!"

Sawyer jolted into action, pulling at the corpse draped over this final person—the smallest body, concealed by another corpse. Not just a body, though. Ilse recognized the voice. She could feel her spine tingling, could feel a renewed energy flushing through her. Just like Dr. Mitchell had taught. Postponing his own emotional reaction for the sake of the client. For the person he was meant to help.

Samantha's voice.

CHAPTER TWENTY

"Samantha?" Ilse said, her tone trembling.

Sawyer grunted, breathing furiously, his muscles training as he hefted the dead body off the final, smallest form lying against the cold concrete.

Her earrings were now missing, but the blonde hair and desperate, frightened gaze were unmistakable.

She was here. They'd found her.

Samantha's killer had found her too…

Dear God. She was breathing. She was breathing! But would she make it? She was injured!

"Samantha!" Ilse yelled, darting in, feeling her own fear fading as she reached out desperately, her fingers gripping Samantha's own frail fingertips.

Ilse's hesitant voice went firm again. A strange, odd sort of courage came over her. Though, perhaps not so much courage as forgetfulness. Forgetfulness at the fear. Forgetfulness at her own emotion, her memories of another basement somewhere else. Her client needed help. This was what she had to do.

Ilse found her hands moving quickly now, the fear fading for a moment as she felt her fingers against cold skin. A shaky cut stretched along Samantha's neck, but down her collarbone instead of her throat.

"He missed me in the dark," Samantha gasped, trembling, her eyes wide, her blonde hair streaked with dirt and sweat and blood. "He missed me… He missed me…" She began to sob, shaking, trembling. "Dr. Beck? Is that you? Dr. Beck—I'm so sorry! I'm so, so sorry!" Samantha was trembling now, sobbing, shaking, covered in dust, blinking against the bright light in her eyes as if she had seen nothing but darkness since she'd gone missing.

Ilse could feel her heart hammering, her pulse racing wildly. She was alive. He'd taken her. But she was alive.

"What did he look like?" Sawyer was saying, sharply. "Is he still here? On the farm?"

"Dr. Beck," Samantha was saying, her fingers wrapping around Ilse's hand, holding so tight it hurt, like a drowning victim clutching a life vest.

There, in a basement of all things, holding her client's hand, Ilse didn't feel so scared anymore. Instead, forgetting her own fear, she forced a smile, a comforting, relaxing smile. "It's going to be okay, Sam. It's all going to be fine. You're safe now. No one's going to hurt you now."

"Is the killer still here?" Sawyer insisted, even more loudly now.

Samantha's eyes fluttered, and she shook her head weakly.

Ilse and Sawyer helped her to her feet. One of her arms draped over Ilse's neck. Her clothing was stained, ripped in places, the cut along her neck still somewhat fresh it seemed, and blood soaked her shirt.

"Doc, get her out of here," Sawyer murmured. "I'm going up to take a look around outside. Don't leave the shack till I come for you, got it?"

Frightened, but hiding it as best she could, staying strong for Sam, Ilse nodded quickly. Then, carefully, Sam's arm draped over her shoulder, Ilse began to move toward the stairs, allowing Samantha to limp at her own, slow, painful pace.

The scent of death lingered everywhere, leached into everything. The scent of rot, of fear.

But Ilse forced herself to take one step at a time, creating arbitrary finish lines in her mind. That piece of straw. Two steps. That discarded wrench. One step. That streak of… of grease. Three steps.

Sawyer's footsteps creaked above as he retreated, moving hastily out to search the farm. Heading toward the farmhouse by the sound of things. Moving off on his own to find the serial killer.

Ilse wasn't built for hunting killers. She preferred tending to those they left behind alive. And so she held Samantha tight, murmuring with each step, just as much for her benefit as her client's. "It's going to all be okay. I promise. You're going to be fine."

Samantha's tears streaked down toward the blood, dripping past her and baptizing the stairs with dark marks against gray, like bullets.

"It's going to be fine. It's all okay. You're safe now. You're safe," Ilse murmured. She walked up the stairs, helping Samantha move. "You're safe. He can't hurt you anymore. I won't let him. He can't hurt any of you anymore…"

For a moment, her vision flickered. Memories surfaced. Ilse found her own tears creeping into her eyes.

"He can't hurt you anymore. I won't let him. He can't. You're safe now," she said. "I promise."

Words she meant with every fiber of her being. Words she wished she'd heard, once upon a time. At least, though, she could share them with someone else.

Samantha's posture was as lumped and shrunken in on herself as ever. But her head wasn't so bowed anymore. Instead it lolled, just about leaning against Ilse. A sort of resigned, but trusting motion. A gesture of exhaustion, but also reliance.

For some reason, this only seemed to strengthen Ilse further and she stepped out of the darkness, moving up the final concrete step, helping Sam into the old dusty shack.

"It's all going to be okay. You're safe now," she murmured.

Ilse meant every word.

She could only hope she wasn't wrong. A killer was still out there. The man who'd murdered the rest of them in the basement. The man who'd taken Samantha…

He was still out there.

Ilse heard the flurry of footsteps, then heard Sawyer's voice shout through the door. "Ambulance is on its way, Doc. She doing all right?"

Ilse cleared her throat. "We're okay. For now. How long for the EMTs?"

"Ten minutes max."

"You see anything? Any sign of him?"

Sawyer emerged back in the doorway, his long, lanky shadow stretching past him into the dark. He shook his head slowly, pressing a hand to hold his baseball cap in place. He frowned, his face dark, his countenance gloomy like the sky. "No sign. Farmhouse is abandoned. Empty. No vehicle either."

Samantha gave a soft little whimper in Ilse's ear. Ilse's stomach twisted in fury and fear.

The killer was still out there.

Perhaps her client wasn't so safe after all.

CHAPTER TWENTY ONE

Ilse watched as the old shack swarmed with paramedics and cops. The row of nails and scattered screws had been swept off the road, and multiple squad cars with flashing lights lined the roundabout at the end of the street beneath the watch of the old, dusty farmhouse.

An ambulance sat with its back doors open, as if preparing to embrace the shack. A stretcher had been removed from the back of the white vehicle, and two paramedics were gently situating Samantha, while at the same time checking her vitals and tending to her wound.

Samantha winced against a sudden hiss of disinfectant against the injury, and her fingers groped out, twisting in Ilse's direction like a child desperate for her mother.

Her eyes were wide with panic, and Ilse hurried over, reaching out and taking the woman's hand in hers.

"He's going to find me again," Samantha whispered. "I know he is. The hospital won't be safe! He's coming for me!"

Ilse shushed her softly, giving Sam's fingers a gentle squeeze. At the same time, though, she didn't disagree. Instead, she glanced toward the farmhouse, where Agent Sawyer and a couple of other police were going through the building for the third time, searching every nook and cranny.

The scowl of frustration on Sawyer's rigid, stony features told the tale.

Not so much as a fingerprint.

Ilse ground her teeth in frustration, moving to the side as one of the paramedics strapped an IV bag up to a metal hanger, inserting the IV into Samantha's arm. She didn't even seem to notice.

"I'm cursed," she was murmuring. "Twice now… Twice…" she whimpered.

Ilse just held her hand, unsure what else to say. One of the paramedics said, quietly, "You're lucky they found you when they did. You might have bled out."

If he'd meant this to be soothing, it only seemed to send Samantha into another round of hyperventilation. Sam squeezed Ilse's fingers until they hurt, and Ilse winced against the grip, but kept her hand in her patient's.

"It's going to be okay, you're safe now," Ilse said, quietly. For her part, she shivered at the paramedic's words. Maybe the killer hadn't made a mistake with his shallow cut across Sam's shoulder, just missing her neck. Maybe he'd intended to leave her like that, in the dark, surrounded by the dead, bleeding out.

She shivered at the sheer horror of it.

"Was it him?" Ilse said, her voice nearly a whisper now. A group of police moved past, banging open the shack's doors and heading inside. "Did you recognize him?"

Sam whimpered at the question, her eyes scrunched up now, her lips barely parted. The paramedics were beginning to move the stretcher, gently guiding it back toward the open ambulance doors.

Ilse walked alongside, still watching her client.

"I don't know, Dr. Beck. I don't. He—he wore a hat. Disguised his voice—spoke low. Sounded like he was a smoker or something," she said, quickly. "I really don't know. But—but he did give me this."

At that, she extricated her fingers delicately from Ilse's grasp and reached with a trembling hand into her pocket. A second later, her fingers reemerged, this time gripping a small, pink Post-it note. Samantha stared at the thing for a moment. "Right before he hit me. He gave me that."

Ilse frowned, delicately taking the piece of paper. On it, at the top, a simple smiley face. Arranged in the same proportions as the bodies in the basement.

Ilse swallowed once, but then read the words on the paper. *Run. I'm going to kill you.*

That was it. Just the two sentences. Ilse reread the note, wrinkling her nose, her eyes glancing up to the smiley face again. Taunting her, no doubt. Mocking his victim. Like a cat playing with a caught mouse. The sadism alone, the desire to evoke fear, was obvious. A psychopathic, sadistic personality, then.

"You couldn't see their face at all?" Ilse said, trying not to press too hard, but feeling her own nerves stretch and strain.

The paramedics had now reached the back of the ambulance and seemed ready to load the stretcher. Samantha was shaking her head. "I didn't see. I don't even know if I'd remember, Dr. Beck. I—I don't know," she sobbed.

"It's okay," Ilse replied quickly. "It's all going to be okay. I promise you. It's going to be fine."

"He's going to find me again. I know he is!"

"So you think it was the same man? Did he use that sort of sticky-note before? The smiley face… Do you remember that?"

Sam paused, shaking her head at first, but then her expression froze. She stared off into the distance, like a doe caught in headlights. She swallowed sharply all of a sudden, and began to whimper, trembling where she lay on the stretcher.

"I don't remember," she said, quickly.

And for a moment, Ilse felt nearly certain Sam was holding something back.

"Are you sure?" she said, gently. "Anything you say can help us find him. There's an FBI agent here. They're really good at catching bad guys. The smiley face. Do you know what it means?"

Again, a wide-eyed look of panic, of desperate recollection, but then a tightening of the lips, a vacant, distant gaze and a quick shake of her head.

Ilse dropped it.

Besides, she wasn't sure she wanted her client's killer to have returned.

Purely for selfish reasons. If Samantha's old tormentor had found her again, what was stopping Ilse's from finding her?

She shivered. A flash of a memory: two mismatched eyes staring in a dark basement. The snap of a bird's wings. The crunch of her finger. A yelp of pain. Sleeping with a lump nestled against her chin. Warm at the start of the night, but cold as it stretched to morning.

Ilse held her breath, counting softly and releasing it at once. Those postcards were from someone. Not Mitchell. Someone who knew her past. Who knew more than they should. Someone had found her. Maybe her father… who else could it be?

At that moment, Ilse heard the sound of crunching dirt, and she whirled back to find Agent Sawyer approaching them, a frown on his face. He brushed a hand through his prematurely silver hair and swallowed as if tasting something sour.

"How's the cut?" he said, directing the question to the paramedics.

"Not too bad," said one. "We can bandage it here. Clean it up. It's mostly superficial. A bleeder, but not dangerous."

Sawyer sighed, crossing his arms over his flannel shirt. "She staying at the hospital?"

One of the paramedics shrugged. "Might be good for observation. Just for the night."

The moment he said it, though, Samantha began to shake. "No," she said, desperately. "No. He'll find me there. I know he will. No! No! No!"

"Ms. Wright," one paramedic said quickly, "please calm down. You'll rip out the IV."

"I'm fine!" she said, desperately. "Don't take me to the hospital. No! No!" Her voice grew even louder, and surrounding police began to glance over.

The paramedics shrugged toward Agent Sawyer.

"You live nearby?" he said.

"I don't want to go home either," Samantha replied, her voice trembling.

Sawyer's eyes flashed with something akin to pity. But just as quickly, he hid it, speaking slowly, gently, his tone neutral, but relentlessly pressing forward. A solution-oriented man, no doubt. An action-oriented fellow.

"Friends, family?" he said, quietly. "You need somewhere safe to stay. We could post a cop at the hospital."

"What will that do!" she yelled. "He'll find me! He'll find me!"

Ilse listened, feeling her own sense of guilt rising. She should have listened to her client the first time around. She should have believed her, instead of writing her off as paranoid. She'd nearly died. She'd been left to bleed out in a room of corpses.

All of it was Ilse's fault.

She'd failed…

Now, as she watched the wide-eyed look of panic, like a spooked mare trapped in a barn, Ilse could feel her conscience jolt. She thought of Dr. Mitchell. Once her own therapist and teacher, now a friend. More than once she'd been to Dr. Mitchell's home for dinner. He kept her safe when she was scared. More than once he'd invited her to join his family for Thanksgiving, for Christmas, for birthdays…

She knew the dangers of getting too close to a client, though. Strange stories. Boundaries best left uncrossed.

But Samantha had given a cry for help, and Ilse had nearly let her get killed.

She felt the guilt, felt the gaping maw of the shack behind her as if the doors themselves wanted to reach out and swallow.

What if Samantha was right again? What if the killer tried to track her down? Ilse glanced at the little sticky note with the smiley face. Then, steeling herself, she looked up.

"I can look after her," Ilse said, softly. "At my place. We're near enough to a hospital in case of an emergency. My place is safe."

The moment she said it, Samantha's eyes widened even further. For a moment, she seemed caught on the edge of panic and relief. She looked at Ilse, staring as if assessing her one last time. Ilse could still feel the way Sam had nestled against her shoulder in the basement. A gesture of trust. The trust of someone with no other options but fear and danger.

Sometimes, all it took was a single friendly shoulder.

"Yes," Ilse said, more insistently. She nodded in an encouraging way to her patient. "You'll be safe there. I'll keep an eye on you. Just for the night, until we can find somewhere else you'll be safe."

At the word *safe*, Samantha gave a soft little shiver of delight. She closed her eyes, as if drifting off for a moment. For the first time since leaving the shack, her fingers weren't trembling so badly.

The paramedics were shaking their heads, frowning.

Sawyer glanced from one to the other. "Does she have to go to a hospital?"

One paramedic sighed, glancing at the IV bag. He looked to her freshly bandaged neck and then shrugged. "I'd highly suggest it."

Samantha's eyes fluttered, and she whimpered, "No," but not so insistently this time. A quiet, tired little protest. A desperate, hopeful plea that someone, anyone, might finally listen.

Ilse couldn't let her client down a second time. She looked Sawyer dead in the eyes. "I'll look after her. Keep an eye on her all night if I have to. We need to find somewhere she'll be safe." Ilse looked to the paramedics. "Do you really think it'll be better for her to stay awake all night in terror, trembling and panicked? I can't imagine that's better."

Again, the paramedics frowned, sighing. But one at a time, they finally seemed to relent with soft little nods.

The one who'd attached the IV shook his head, muttering, "I suppose I'll call the hospital. I'll need clearance…"

"You have my clearance," Sawyer interrupted. "She'll be safe with the doc. Do what you have to. How much time?"

"Maybe twenty minutes," said the paramedic. He gestured at the IV bag. "Should be enough. I really have to insist, though, Ms. Wright. The hospital is very safe. We have—"

"No," Samantha said, releasing the single word with a gusting breath as if it had taken every last ounce of strength. Then, silently, she shook her head, her blonde, dirty hair shifting against the pillow.

"You heard her," Ilse said, looking hard at Sawyer. "I will keep an eye on her." *This time.* "I promise."

Agent Sawyer glanced over at the old shack, his eyes trailing along the dirt road before returning to Samantha. "All right. Make sure she's safe. And keep that dumb phone of yours near at hand." With that, he turned toward the police officers who were reemerging from the shack, accompanied by a coroner's assistant.

All of them looked grim-faced.

Sawyer gestured at two of the cops. "You, and you, with me. Check the woods."

"We already did."

"Do it again. With me."

Sawyer stalked off like a hound with a scent, and the indicated police officers fell dutifully into line behind him, moving around the shack, toward the woods in search of the missing killer.

As they moved, Ilse felt a shiver up her spine. If the killer had come for Samantha twice, what was stopping him from striking a third time?

CHAPTER TWENTY TWO

"You're sure you're all right to move around like that?" Ilse said, allowing her voice to carry concern.

"I'm fine," Samantha murmured, wincing as she stepped barefoot through the house. Every so often she would glance toward a window, or pause by the front door and check to make sure it was locked. The plastic bag she'd used to cover her bandages while showering was visible over the edge of the trash can by the sink.

Dusk had fallen, and Ilse sat at her kitchen table, watching Samantha. Her client hobbled on her feet, rubbing at the thick bandages along the base of her neck. Sam's hair was wet from the shower, and she now wore a change of clothes Ilse had loaned her.

A cup of tea sat across the kitchen table, cooling where it sat neglected on its coaster. Small little strands of steam wafted from the glass, streaking the window over the table with mist.

"We're safe," Ilse called from the kitchen as she listened to the rattle of the patio door. "No one is going to get to us. There's going to be a patrol car in the neighborhood, too." Even as she said it, though, she wasn't sure she believed it. Ilse winced, feeling her pounding headache brought on by sheer exhaustion. Her eyes ached, and she wanted nothing more than to collapse in her bed and drift off.

But not yet—not now. Was it true? Were they really safe? Samantha's killer was still out there. Twice, he'd gone after her. What would stop another attempt?

Ilse shivered at the thought, rubbing her nose and inhaling deeply if only to oxygenate her blood stream.

Samantha came back into the kitchen, wincing again, and then slumping into her seat, inhaling the steam from her cup of tea, her eyes wide as she stared at the table. At the same time, her shoulders were heavy, her head bowed as if exhausted.

"You can take the bed if you'd like," Ilse said, quietly. "I've already made up the couch."

"No. No, Dr. Beck. The couch is fine. Really. Thank you. You've been too kind already." Samantha's voice cracked briefly, but then she glanced off, inhaling more steam from the cup of tea. "I… I was so scared," she said, her voice shaking. "I just froze up." She looked up now, her eyes bleary, whether from tears or the steam, Ilse wasn't sure.

Sam shook her head in a quick jolting motion. "When I called you… When he came up behind me. I just stared. I didn't even run. I was frozen to the ground."

"It wasn't your fault," Ilse murmured.

"No… No, but it was. I didn't do anything, Dr. Beck! Nothing!" Samantha's hand tightened around the tea mug all of a sudden.

"Careful, that's hot."

Samantha didn't let go, her teeth set.

"Sam, it's going to be all right," Ilse said, quietly. "There's nothing you could have done." She reached out and gently pulled Sam's fingers from the mug.

For a moment, Ilse paused, frowning. She thought she heard a gentle knock on the door. But when she listened, all she could hear was the rustling of trees outside the window.

Samantha finally released her grip. But her other hand had clenched into a fist, and she pressed it to the table. In a ghost of a whisper, she murmured, "I should have done something… I—I should have fought back. Anything. Both times, I didn't do anything, Dr. Beck. I just let him—let him…" She shivered and glanced off.

Ilse patted Sam's hand again. "You were a child the first time. He snuck up on you this time."

"I didn't even *run*! I didn't fight. I was so helpless, so scared…" Sam closed her eyes. "I promised myself, if I ever faced him again, I'd *do* something. I'd fight back. Protect myself. Even… even if it meant…" She glanced off and sniffed. "Even if it ended for me. At least I would have *done* something, you know?"

Ilse tried to console Sam, but inwardly, her own mind was whirring.

She *did* know. Knew more than Sam even realized. She pictured the two postcards. Hilda Mueller. Someone taunting her. Pictured the surfacing memories, repressed, hidden. Memories she had long since forgotten, long since buried deep beneath shovel after shovel of neglect and willful ignorance.

Memories that refused to stay buried, as if washed free by a storm.

Someone was hunting her too. It was as if fate had aligned. As if, like Dr. Mitchell often said, his clients' lives mirrored his own life. Small truths were often hidden in the places where one might help another. Dr. Mitchell often claimed he learned just as much from his clients as they did from him. Just as much from his students. She wasn't sure she'd ever believed him before…

But now…

Nothing could be more true of Samantha's returning tormentor.

Ilse could feel, even now, eyes fixed on her. Something, or *someone*, hidden somewhere watching her, stalking her. She wondered if this was how Sam felt. Ilse had thought her client had been paranoid. Ilse had dismissed the woman's cry for help. She'd failed to act.

And now there Sam sat, a bandage around her neck, her voice trembling. She'd been left in a room of corpses. Left to bleed out among the dead. The killer, it seemed, had wanted her to suffer the most. Wanted her fear, as if he'd been feasting on the terror itself.

Ilse shivered and closed her eyes for the briefest moment. She found her own hand curling on the table. Found it forming a fist.

She remembered the way she'd stood rooted to the spot at the top of the basement back in the shack. She hadn't even been able to step into the dark.

Like a child all over again. Like a helpless, defenseless little girl.

Ilse felt her finger pressing to the missing lobe of her maimed right ear. She brushed her hair forward for a moment.

"Is that a scar?" Sam murmured softly, her voice sleepy.

Ilse blinked her eyes open and realized her client was peering at Ilse's missing earlobe.

"It's nothing," she said, reflexively. "Are you sure I can't get you something to eat? I have some granola. It's homemade. I'm afraid I haven't gone shopping in a while."

"I… I don't really like granola. Sorry," Samantha said. "I know how spoiled that makes me sound. You've done more than enough. Way more."

"No, that's fine," Ilse said, quickly. She flashed a placating smile. Even then, though, she could feel the way her fist had curled.

She resonated with Sam's desire to fight back. But how did one fight shadows? How did one stave off fear itself? A cowardly, slinking enemy. A corruption that seeped through the imagination, hunted its victims in dreams and memories.

Ilse didn't know how to even start fighting back.

She didn't blame Samantha for going still, freezing in place. Didn't blame her for falling to stop the abductor a second time.

Was it the same hunter from her past? Was it the same monster from Samantha's childhood?

Her client's history mirrored her own in such alarming ways.

Different countries, different kidnappers, but similar trauma. Similar memories long since buried, slowly surfacing.

Ilse slowly released her hand, rolling her fingers until her knuckles stretched.

"I… I could eat," Samantha murmured.

"What would you like?" Ilse asked.

"Umm. Maybe pizza?"

Ilse smiled and nodded. "There's a local place nearby. They usually deliver late."

Samantha flashed a smile, her cheeks dimpling. An expression so rare for the young woman. An expression like a sunrise against a gloomy sky.

Ilse felt warmth in her chest at the small, simple gesture of joy. One could never underestimate the impact pizza could have on someone's mood.

"Pepperoni?"

"Sure. Whatever you want. Umm…" Samantha winced. "I hate to ask. But would you mind extra cheese?"

Ilse clicked her tongue in mock severity, but was already fishing out her dumb phone. "Perfect," she said, getting to her feet and moving toward the small cupboard where she kept the local menus and brochures dropped off at her door from the eateries and restaurants in the area.

She could feel Samantha watching her, as she placed the order for the pie. Twelve-inch, extra cheese and pepperoni. And two ranch dipping cups.

Ilse would have to spend an extra hour at the gym when she got a chance. But tonight was a good night to treat herself.

"Will that be all?" the voice on the other end said.

"That's it," said Ilse. "What time?"

"You can pick it up in twenty-five minutes. Thank you!"

"Wait," Ilse said, quickly. "I want delivery."

The voice on the other end spoke apologetically. "Oh, I'm sorry. I thought I was clear. Delivery is done for the night. Only pickup. Would you like me to cancel the order?"

Ilse began to nod and reply, but then she paused, glancing at Samantha. She pictured the woman's smile. Pictured the eager look on her face at the thought of something so simple as dough and cheese and sauce. Samantha could wait back at the house—safe and sound behind locked doors. It couldn't hurt, could it? Maybe it was just her sleep-deprived state making rough decisions.

Ilse sighed. "Where are you guys again?"

"Just on the corner of Creswell and Priva."

Ilse paused for a moment, closing her eyes and picturing the drive. It was only five minutes away. Not so far… Was it?

She glanced again at Samantha, feeling the weight of the day heavy against her shoulders. Feeling the threats and whispers of fear taunting and niggling in her mind.

Ilse felt her fist bunch up again. Five minutes away to get Samantha her pizza. Five minutes was nothing. Ilse could be brave for five minutes. So could Samantha. They would reward themselves with pepperoni and double cheese.

"No, that's fine," Ilse said, quickly. "I'll be there."

Samantha watched quizzically as Ilse lowered her phone, shaking her head apologetically. "Delivery is done for the night," she explained. Samantha's face fell. "But they're only five minutes away. I figured I'd go pick it up. Would you like to come with?"

Sam's expression brightened again. She paused, glancing nervously around the house. "I'll show you how to lock up," Ilse said, instinctively. "It'll be fine. If you'd rather I call and cancel, though, I totally understand."

But Samantha was shaking her head, breathing slowly, but nodding to herself in a sort of quiet determination. "Five minutes is nothing," she said.

"Nothing," Ilse replied. "Exactly."

She glanced at her dumb phone, checking the clock. Five minutes. Twenty-five for it to be ready. She checked when she'd placed the call. Eleven exactly. Eleven-twenty, then. That's when she'd leave. Not a second before, or after. One had to be precise with things so fickle as time.

She nodded, watching the digital clock on her old flip phone.

Eleven twenty. Exactly. Precisely.

Ilse could still feel the way her feet had glued to the stairs at the top of the basement. Could feel the crippling, freezing fear paralyzing her. She set her jaw, eyes narrowed. Never again. She refused. Not this time… Not again.

You're not thinking clearly, said a small voice in her mind. A voice that sounded surprisingly similar to Dr. Mitchell's.

But Ilse ignored it. What could a little trip to get some pizza hurt anyway? That's all she wanted, wasn't it? Just to pick up a pizza? What else could she possibly want? What else was there?

Samantha would be safe, locked inside, behind doors and shuttered windows. Cops were patrolling the neighborhood. She could take the bedroom, and lock that door as well.

She'd be safe. She had to be.

Ilse nodded to herself, checking the phone again.

Eleven twenty precisely.

Then she'd go pick up a pizza. Nothing more. Not a single thing.

***

She gripped the steering wheel to the Boat as she headed toward town, her eyes on the road, her breathing steady. Her knuckles were white against the leather, and she could feel the faint puff of her breath against her upper lip.

No one on the road behind her. No one in front.

She knew the drive by heart. She pulled to a red light in the dark of night. No other cars at the intersection. None on the road at all that she could see.

Samantha was back at the house, locked in. Safe, protected. Ilse had even passed the police officer who'd been sent to babysit the old, lonely road outside the lake.

She glanced to the right. There, down the street, she spotted the glowing, fluorescent sign for the late night pizza parlor. Her mouth watered briefly as she stared at the place.

The light turned green.

She didn't move. For a moment, she sat idling in her car, beneath the bright green light, staring across the street. The pizza parlor was to the right…

Her eyes, though, trailed in the other direction.

Her fingers closed around the steering wheel, knuckles white and bunched much like a fist. Her breathing came more pronounced … more labored.

Only five minutes to get the food. Five minutes to get back…

Samantha was safe and sound. Watched by a cop…

What was another five minutes anyway? Just a bit longer out in the night… A bit longer…

Ilse could still hear Samantha's trembling voice. The fear in her words. Her desperate regret at not having done *anything.* She hadn't run. She hadn't fought.

She'd simply been hunted down by her past and victimized a second time.

Ilse felt a jolt of fury at this very thought.

She refused to let it happen to her. Not again. The postcards… someone was sending the postcards. Someone was drawing nearer. Someone knew who she was… Knew her past.

She refused to be caught frozen. Not again. Not like at the top of those stairs back in the shack, frozen in place. Helpless, useless, desperate like some frightened little child. A victim.

Ilse could feel her breath quickening.

She knew what Donovan Mitchell would say. She knew what she would advise a client. She knew what she was about to do was very, very stupid.

But could she live with herself if she didn't? She refused to live as a coward. She couldn't do it. It would eat her to pieces if she did. Samantha's killer was out there, hiding again. Hunting, stalking. Samantha was behind closed doors, safe.

But Ilse's own history… the monster from her past…

He was out there somewhere too. Someone was, at the very least. Someone who *knew.*

And maybe… instead of waiting for him to come to her… Ilse swallowed, wetting her lips, feeling her throat dry all of a sudden.

Maybe she should go to him.

What was another five minutes… Just five minutes…

The pizza parlor was to the right.

She turned left, pulling through the intersection. Even as she did, she half paused, wondering if perhaps she ought to just grab the food and go. But then, feeling a flicker of frustration, she floored the gas, pulling away even more quickly to the left. Moving back away from the town. Moving in the direction of the old mountain road.

Where the two bodies had been found.

Where the killer had been active.

The same back road where Samantha had been abducted. Ilse picked up the pace, zipping through the night now, moving rapidly toward the mountains, toward the old forest. The skies were dark. Impossible to tell if they were overcast or simply black as tar. Ilse only had eyes for the road.

In, out, she breathed softly. "Holmes, two hundred possible victims. Deceased. Dissociative disorder."

She wouldn't cower. She refused to hide. She floored the pedal now, teeth set, determination falling over her like a warm liquid. *Don't be stupid,* a small voice whispered. Again, it sounded so much like Dr. Mitchell.

But Ilse knew what she was doing. She couldn't turn back. Not now. She'd already made up her mind. If her memories were coming back, if her history was hoping to hunt her again… this time, it wouldn't find a helpless, scared little girl. This time, she'd fight back.

Fingers tight, knuckles white, she tore up the old road and didn't stop until she reached a familiar stretch of highway. Sleep deprived. Check. PTSD triggers. Check. Classic textbook conditioned response. She knew she should have stayed back, knew this was a risk… But sometimes, even the best textbooks held the lousiest advice.

At least, to a sleep-deprived, fear-addled brain.

Ilse pulled sharply off onto the shoulder, watching as another car zipped by in the other direction. She winced against the flash of bright headlights, and then pulled to a complete stop. She parked the car, sitting on the dusty shoulder, facing the small jogger's trail that led into the woods.

The trail seemed an invitation all of a sudden, a beckoning, dark portal into some other realm.

Ilse breathed softly, exhaling in, out, quiet.

This was where Samantha had been kidnapped.

She hadn't fought back. She hadn't even run.

Could Ilse do any better? Was she even capable?

Trembling, she slowly pushed open the Boat's door, stepping out onto the dusty shoulder. The highway was abandoned again. The sound of the only other vehicle had faded. Now, in the chill night, beneath the trees, surrounded by the woods and dust and asphalt and concrete, Ilse felt a flicker of anxiety in her chest.

Slowly, she pulled her phone out. She cycled to the newest number she'd stored.

Agent Sawyer. With shaking fingers, she sent a text message. Then she put her phone back in her pocket and approached the jogger's trail.

She stood by the concrete barrier, facing the old, dark road cutting into the deeper portion of forest, into the black and darkness. Into shadow.

Her feet stood frozen for a moment. The same way they had at the top of the stairs back at the shack. What was another five minutes? Just a little more time…

Samantha was safe. Everyone was safe. It was all going to be okay…

Ilse swallowed once. She refused to cower. Not again. She wasn't a little child anymore. She nodded once to herself. *Don't be stupid...*

She ignored the voice, though, and, dragging her feet from the concrete, she stepped off the shoulder and onto the old trail. Then she began to walk, moving hastily along the dusty road, eyes fixed ahead, arms like pistons.

She marched into the old woods, away from the highway, away from her parked car, away from it all and toward fear itself.

Ilse wasn't a child anymore.

CHAPTER TWENTY THREE

"Vicarious resolution to trauma," Ilse murmured softly, answering the thoughts reverberating in her mind. "Projecting interpersonal control on tangential issues." Dust and dirt crunched beneath her feet as she took the trail, following it along the old concrete barriers lining the nighttime road. "Stupid," she added at last, channeling her inner Agent Sawyer. "Really, really stupid."

The streets were empty; the night stretched above and stared down, watchful of the vacant trails. Ilse rubbed at her arms, feeling a chill seep through the soft fabric of her baggy hoodie.

This was not a good idea. How had a quick trip for a bite to eat turned into something so stupid?

And yet, even as she thought it, she continued marching on, eyes ahead, taking the portion of the dirt road that ran parallel to the highway itself, on the other side of the concrete barrier.

A trained psychologist. A licensed therapist. And yet, still, she ignored her own counsel—maybe she'd been too hard on some of her patients over the years. The ones who'd ignored her completely and beaten their own path.

She shivered, remembering how some of those stories had ended.

But still, she marched along the old dirt road, arms at her side now, swinging like pendulums. It had been a while since she'd gotten some decent cardio in. She picked up the pace a bit, speed-walking and breathing in slow, steady patterns.

Fear was a liar. Fear was her enemy. Sometimes, it seemed, even more than her history, her father—even more than Hilda Mueller's memories. Fear was the true threat.

Stupid though this was, a small part of her felt like this was the only way… No more cowering behind locked doors and shuttered windows. No more double- and triple-checking locks… well, perhaps that would be a harder habit to break. But she refused for fear to be the motivator now. Refused to allow it to control and manipulate as it so often did.

As she stalked along the old road, the same road the killer had been hunting, the same road where two women had been killed, where Samantha had been kidnapped, she could feel the fear rising like a cloud over her. Despite her best intentions, despite her desire to face it head on, fear was stretching across her like a blanket, weighing her movements, suppressing her thoughts, strangling the life from every moment of natural vitality, trying to drown her in sheer panic.

"No," Ilse said, simply. "No!" she repeated, louder into the dark.

Headlights suddenly flashed over the top of the hill, moving down past the concrete barrier. Ilse's heart skipped a beat. She waited, breathing heavily, watching as the car slid past. For a moment, it almost seemed to stall, the engine grumbling loudly in the night, echoing and reverberating off the concrete barrier. But then the headlights shifted, and the vehicle picked up the pace again, growling and speeding away.

Ilse breathed a bit easier, watching the taillights blink back toward her like the red eyes of some sentinel demon.

Where had the other bodies come from?

She stopped moving for a second, standing on the old dusty trail, frowning to herself. The FBI was tracking down the identities of the other victims they'd found in that basement.

Ilse shivered.

Where had they come from? This road too? More hitchhikers? More unsuspecting victims?

Ilse gritted her teeth and shook her head, marching forward again. *Take captive every thought...* She mouthed the phrase, picking up her pace until she was jogging now, kicking up dust and darting under the splayed branches and shivering shadows across the dusty road.

Another car's lights flashed behind her, this one coming from the opposite direction. Again, the vehicle seemed to slow…

Ilse paused, looking back. Her heart skipped a beat, watching as the car moved through the gap between the opposite highways. It paused beneath a clearly marked No-U-turn sign.

A cop?

Not a cop. No, a truck. An old, flatbed truck. It came across three empty lanes, pulling from the sheer opposite side of the highway and coming to a crunching halt next to the barrier.

The headlights illuminated her, shining bright, and Ilse could feel the oppressive cloud of fear now turn into a cold trickle rattling down her spine. For a moment, breathing heavily, she came to another halt, facing the bright lights, squinting against the glare, listening to the steady rumble of the truck's engine.

A second later, the lights clicked off, and a hand waved out of the front driver's side.

“H—hello?” Ilse said, hesitantly, staring toward the waving, fluttering hand.

“Need a ride?” a voice called from inside the truck. A faint, gravelly voice, like a smoker’s. Hard to make out, though.

Ilse could feel her feet rooted to the spot, could feel the familiar chill rising up her spine. Her mind flashed with images of basements and postcards and dead pigeons. Her teeth set and she stared at the greasy windshield.

The fear was slowly met by a rising sense of sheer fury. Righteous indignation that went as deep as her bones.

The man’s outline was hard to determine through the windshield. Though it looked like he might have been wearing a baseball cap. For a moment, Ilse thought of Agent Tom Sawyer. For another moment, she felt a shiver of surprise at how much she missed the lanky, silver-haired BAU agent. Missed him, and especially his gun.

Alone on the open highway, witnessed only by the moon, Ilse forced one frozen foot forward. Her hands trembled horribly as she did, but she refused to back down now. She was here for a reason. No more postcards, no more haunting memories. She wasn’t a little girl anymore.

“Hi,” Ilse said, finding her voice surprisingly steady despite her inner turmoil. “Can I help you?”

The same road. The same road the killer had been hunting. The same road.

Ilse blinked and watched as the man in the baseball cap gave a soft little chuckle. It smelled, perhaps, like cigarette smoke wafting from the front of the vehicle. “Thought maybe I could help you,” he called back.

Ilse shivered, rubbing her elbows through her thick sweater. She shifted uncomfortably on the road, feeling trapped for a moment. Her hand went to her pocket, where she’d placed her keys, and she felt the comforting, hefty weight of the ring of metal. She paused, though, hesitant. Where was her pepper spray?

She glanced down, frowning. The little plastic container was missing. Where had it gone?

She froze now, double-checking her pocket, then her keys. The pepper spray was missing. Panic began to set in. Her sheer exhaustion weighed heavy, and the momentum of her choices up to this moment pressed on her.

Abort. She needed to abort. This was a terrible idea. Unarmed, defenseless…

Her hand tightened around the keys, and she took another step toward the truck despite her thoughts.

“Just saw your car back that way,” the man said, waving a hand over his shoulder. “Did you break down?”

Ilse swallowed once. “Yes,” she lied. *Leave! Get out of there!* But she ignored her subconscious. She’d come too far. She was too tired to try again. Sometimes risks were necessary. Besides… she had a plan, didn’t she?

She swallowed, hand tightening further around the keys. Where had she lost her pepper spray?

“Tough luck. Well, wanted to be a good citizen. Need a lift anywhere? I’m in no rush.”

Ilse exhaled slowly. What sort of folk were in no rush at midnight? Most, perhaps. But on the other hand, what sort of folk pulled over to the side of the road at midnight for a stranger? The man seemed friendly enough, though his voice came muffled from the front of the cabin, and his hand—which still dangled out the window—seemed limp.

But still… Ilse hadn’t come here for fear. Just five minutes. Always five minutes. What could it hurt? The keys were good enough, weren’t they? She’d defended herself with far less as a child. She could only imagine the absolute gold strike a set of keys would have been back in that basement.

“Unknown… Brown eyes… Six victims…”

“What was that?”

“Nothing. Yeah, I could use a ride. Thanks!” She’d said it. She’d committed. Damn it.

Ilse circled to the passenger side of the truck. Before she could reach the handle, she heard the click of locks, and the driver reached across, shoving the door open. His smile flashed beneath a baseball cap, his features wreathed in shadow as he waved at her, gesturing for her to get in. A very pronounced smile. Almost an intentional thing. More a leer than anything.

Ilse, though, refused to allow her feet to command her actions. When they again seemed intent on rooting to the concrete, she forced herself up the small metal rung into the front of the truck, and slid into the passenger side. Inside the cabin it was surprisingly clean. She detected the faint scent of air freshener, trying to hide the odor of cigarette smoke.

“Mind shutting that?” the man said.

Ilse nodded numbly. *Stupid! Don't be stupid! Stupid! Don't be stupid!* She ignored her own thoughts and shut the door. A second later, the lock clicked.

"Sorry," the man said. "Locks are finicky." He brushed off any chance at anxiety with a wink and another smile. "Where can I take you?" he asked.

The man's chin was covered in stubble, and he smelled of smoke and lavender from the air freshener. Two little dice dangled from his mirror, cottony, fluffy things. In the rearview mirror, Ilse noticed two strange canisters sitting on the back seat and… there, tucked beneath the canisters, she spotted what looked like the hilt of a bowie knife.

She swallowed, glancing toward the locked door, her fingers trailing down the cool glass, touching against the metal handle inside the cabin.

But she'd come this far. No backing out now.

The same road. Don't be stupid. The same road. Don't be stupid.

She ignored the thoughts again. "Oh, just to Three Lakes," she said. "That work for you?"

"Dandy," the man said with a nod and a wink. "Buckle up."

He waited expectantly, a sort of hungry look in his eyes as she reached with a quavering hand toward the buckle past her shoulder and then pulled it, locking it in place. Alone, trapped, watched by a stranger with just a bit *too* much eagerness.

She felt like a specimen, the way Dr. Mitchell sometimes made her feel. But where Donovan's attention was on her behalf, examining to help, to aid and care for, this man's attention seemed of an entirely different and far more selfish variety.

Once she was buckled, the truck began to move, heading in the exact opposite direction it had been going before, taking her back toward town.

"Kinda late to be out on your own, isn't it?" the man asked in a light, airy tone.

Ilse's eyes fixed on the road. "Wanted some fresh air," she murmured.

"Know what's wrong with your car?"

"I'm not really a car person."

"Oh… Well, I am. I can take a look if you'd like."

Ilse swallowed. "No… No, that's fine. If you could just take me back to town."

"Sure, sure, whatever you want." He shot her a sidelong glance, his eyes lingering on her face for a moment and then shifting down, taking more of her in.

Ilse stiffened in her seat, locked in place, feeling like an animal in a zoo, trapped in a cage.

"You know, I don't do this for just anyone," the man said, still conversationally. "I had somewhere to be—the opposite direction actually. But, you know, I suppose I can help a fellow citizen out." He reached over and patted her on the leg. His hand lingered for a bit longer.

She glanced in the rearview mirror again, her eyes on the hilt of what she was certain was a bowie knife. She pictured the way he'd smiled, leering as she'd entered his truck. A smile on the top of a note paper. A smile of corpses. A smile from a driver who picked her up on the same road where two women had been killed.

Though she felt like she was doing something monumentally stupid… And it was that. Stupid. She also wasn't an idiot. She knew when a coincidence became more than that.

She shivered as his hand trailed from her thigh.

"Thank you for the ride," she said, stiffly. "You know… Maybe if you just let me off here, I can walk."

"What? No, don't be silly. All sorts of strange guys are out this time of night. A pretty little thing like you? It's just five minutes that way. I've got you." The easy, carefree tone had grown sort of strained now. The man was breathing a bit heavier, his eyes hooded beneath his cap as he stared at the road.

Ilse's fingers pressed against her ring of keys, holding them tight, bunched up in her hand nearest the door. Her thigh felt slick and oily and gross from where his fingers had trailed. Maybe he was just being friendly? Maybe he was just a bit too touchy… Was it all in her head?

The man was whistling softly now, fiddling with the radio, turning the station to a crooning love ballad. It came crackling and low over the car's janky speakers.

"There we go, that's the right mood, yeah?" He chuckled a bit as the love song echoed in the cabin. A prickle spread along Ilse's arms. She glanced toward the locked door again.

"Where you from—you never even told me your name," he said, speaking a bit louder now. Instead of friendly and curious, it came across as demanding.

She shifted. "Ilse," she said.

"Ilse. My ex was named Ilse, you know." He let out a little

shuddering breath accompanied by a wiggle of his thick shoulders against seat leather. “She had a mouth on her, I’ll tell you. A real, real pretty mouth. If you catch my drift…” He glanced at her, his eyes lingering on her lips. This time, he didn’t even try to look away, but instead met her gaze and winked.

“Hey,” he said suddenly. “I gotta take a leak. You can watch if you like.” He gave a grunting little laugh. “Just hang tight one sec, all right?” He pulled the truck sharply over to the side of the road, moving to a rest stop with a blacked out safety light. The truck trundled over asphalt and loose gravel, crunching in its path behind a low grove and against a metal rail blocking the rest stop from the rest of the road.

“What are you doing?” Ilse said, quickly.

“I gotta piss,” he replied, waving a hand dismissively. “Won’t take but a second. I never do. Sit tight, won’t you?”

And then they pulled to a full stop in the darkest, most hidden section of the rest stop, shielded by a metal railing and low trees from the rest of the highway.

The man put the vehicle in park, and—for a moment—it seemed like he was double-checking the doors were locked. Then, smiling, he turned to face her.

CHAPTER TWENTY FOUR

Ilse could feel her heart in her throat. Her pulse quickened under the ogling gaze of the truck driver. "I'm not comfortable," she said, softly.

"Ah, come on. No need to be like that," he replied, watching her with an unblinking gaze from beneath his baseball cap.

Ilse glanced in the mirror, looking over her shoulder, swallowing.

"Hey, so it was really nice of me to stop and pick you up, right?" the man said, quietly. "Really nice," he repeated, emphasizing the words.

Her heart hammered. This was him. This was the guy, and this was what she'd wanted. Stupid. So stupid. But intended. Her voice cracked, caught between terror and anticipation. "Unlock the doors."

"I will. Of course I will. What do you think—I'm some sort of creep? Nah… Look, just—it gets lonely out at night, driving around. You said you were out for some air. Some exercise too, yeah?" He nodded, watching her, his face illuminated faintly by the moon alone, his shadowed features strained and rigid. His breathing had become more like a pant.

Ilse reached for the lock. But he suddenly reached out as well, snaring her fingers.

"Now, hang on!" he said. His grip was tight, painful. "Look. I just want a little bit of exercise myself. We can both get what we want. Your lips are a lot like my ex's. Come here… No, stop—come closer!"

He squeezed hard, crushing her fingers and trying to drag her near him. At that moment, Ilse's other hand ripped from her pocket and she yelled, racking the ring of sharp keys across the man's face. He howled like a wounded cat, letting go all of a sudden and reeling back, reaching up and grasping at his cheek and eye. "Bitch!" he yelled.

Ilse pulled the lock and kicked open the door. The man wasn't done though. Bleeding from the gash along his eye, he unbuckled and scrambled after her, his fingers grabbing at the sleeve of her sweater.

"Come here!" he yelled. A bully, a bastard—just like they all were. The ones who sent her clients. The ones who created them. She felt a jolt of sheer rage at his words, of satisfaction at the blood streaking his face. Her hand bunched again, wrapping around the keys.

Just then, there came a sudden whining noise, followed by a flash of red and blue.

Ilse pulled up, gasping, pushing the man's fingers from her sleeve and retreating to the side of the metal divider.

She watched as the unmarked police car pulled sharply into the rest stop, skidding on the asphalt-strewn ground and coming to a full halt.

"Took you long enough!" Ilse yelled at the top of her lungs, bending over and putting her hands on her knees while gasping at the ground.

A long, lanky form pulled from the front driver's side. Ilse heard the man in the truck curse. She watched him scramble back across the seat, desperately trying to put the truck in gear again.

Sawyer sprinted around the side of the truck. He didn't speak, didn't shout. Just ran, yanked at the door handle, pulling it open. The trucker tried to kick out, yelling and cursing, but Sawyer caught his leg and pulled hard, heaving the driver from the front seat and sending him sprawling to the asphalt.

Sawyer looked over now, his silhouette outlined in the darkness by the whir of blue and red from his sedan.

"Hurt?" he asked her.

She shook her head, trembling. "No… No I'm fine. He has a knife in the back seat."

The trucker groaned, trying to speak and rise to his feet, but Sawyer planted a boot in his chest and sent him sprawling again.

The agent glanced back at Ilse again, expressionless, tongue in his cheek. "Stupid," he said simply.

Ilse gasped. "I… I know," she said in a trembling voice. "At least you got my text. Didn't think it would take you so long to get here."

"Mhmm." Sawyer turned his attention back to the trucker, who was reaching into his pocket as if to pull something. "Don't," the FBI agent cautioned, raising a boot again.

Reluctantly, the trucker's hand retreated from his pocket. The man cursed and spluttered, spittle trailing from his lip to the ground. Sawyer reached down, ripped the baseball cap from the man's head, and tossed it off into the woods. He gripped the man's jaw hard, looking him in the eyes. Then in a quiet, cold voice, Sawyer said, simply, "I know what you look like now."

Ilse shivered at the ice in those words. She wasn't quite sure what he meant by it, but the trucker looked frightened enough.

"She wanted a ride!" the man protested, desperately. "She begged for it! I wasn't doing anything!"

"Mhmm. Get up."

"No—what—she attacked me! Look at my face. Look!"

Sawyer glanced at the cuts from the keys along the side of the man's eye. He looked at Ilse carefully. "He touch you?" he said.

"He tried to grab me, so I hit him," Ilse said quickly. "Self-defense."

Sawyer glanced back at the trucker. "You touch her?" Still calm, still in control, still a looming, lanky shadow stretched across the ground like some scarecrow. Ilse realized a thing about scarecrows: they were designed to frighten, to warn and to guard.

The trucker was frightened enough. He shook his head. "Never laid a finger on her. Not one. That stinky whore? Why would—"

Sawyer kicked him hard in the ribs. The man gasped, wheezing, and then was yanked to his feet, his hands jerked roughly behind his back.

"Under arrest," Sawyer muttered quietly. And that was it. He cuffed the man, then shoved him roughly toward the sedan parked perpendicular to the truck. As he passed Ilse again, he murmured, once more, "Stupid idea."

"It worked," she retorted.

For a moment, she thought she saw the silver-haired agent grin and tug at the brim of his baseball cap as he pushed the wheezing trucker past her. "Mhmm."

She watched as he leveraged the man into the back of the car. Ilse found she could breathe a bit easier now, found that the breeze along the highway felt lighter, more airy. Found, even now, that her feet weren't so stuck to the ground. Her memories weren't so haunting.

There was something about facing one's fears… Something about coming out on top. About fighting back.

Stupid, perhaps. But strangely necessary, if she was honest with herself.

Besides, stupid or not, she'd caught the killer. Ilse watched as Sawyer returned to the front seat of his sedan, glancing at her. He waved a hand in her direction. "Need a ride back to your car?" he muttered.

For the second time that night, Ilse paused, considering the same request. But then she nodded once. "Yeah… Yeah, that'd be great."

This time, as she sidled into the front seat, she didn't feel fear at all. The trucker, doubled over, gasping, and cuffed in the back seat, didn't seem so threatening at all anymore. His truck's lights were still on, the key in the ignition.

"Should we turn it off?" Ilse said, pointing at the vehicle. "The battery might die."

"Mhmm."

Sawyer pulled out of the rest stop, clicking off the whirring blue and red lights and guiding his vehicle along the road, back in the direction of her car.

***

Ilse peered through the gap in the open doorway of the interrogation room. Sawyer braced the door for a second, listening and watching as Sergeant Faber and another police officer pushed their suspect roughly into one of the chairs. His hands were still cuffed, and he was muttering furiously about police abuse, demanding a lawyer.

Beneath the bright lights, away from the darkened roads and the shadowed brim of his cap, the man wasn't nearly so scary. He was young, for a start… Even younger than Ilse, by the look of things.

"Got it?" Sawyer called into the room.

Sergeant Faber flashed a thumbs-up in his direction, but then returned her attention to the suspect, giving just as good as she got. "Shut it," she said, growling. "We found your knife. Your truck is being impounded as we speak."

"He hit me!" the young man yelled. "That douchebag hit me!" He jutted his jaw toward Sawyer. Long, slick strands of oily hair tumbled past the man's face. He even had a smattering of acne along his chin.

Ilse stood behind Sawyer, watching through the doorway as the man shook and twisted beneath the bright lights. Gone was the ominous, predatory leer. Gone were the innuendo and asinine remarks. Gone were the ogling and the panting breaths.

Now, the young man was whining like a child, shaking his greasy hair from side to side as he desperately pleaded his case, like a scolded kid.

Sawyer stepped away from the door now, allowing it to slowly shut, and he turned to face Ilse, quiet as ever, just watching her.

"He's younger than I thought," Ilse said softly. The door finally clicked shut behind the BAU operative.

"Mhmm."

Ilse sighed. "Means he's probably a different killer than the one from twenty years ago who abducted Samantha." As she said it, she found this offered her some strange semblance of relief. It took a moment for her to realize why, but then it registered. If Samantha's boogeyman had stayed in the dark archives of her past, then maybe Ilse could expect the same…

Maybe the postcards were just someone's idea of a sick joke. Someone from the town. Someone who may have accidentally recognized her. Maybe nothing more. The trucker was too young to have been the same abductor from all those years ago. He was a new, upstart killer, haunting the mountain roads in search of prey as indicated by his treatment of Ilse. But not the old ghost hidden in a closet or basement. Not Samantha's tormentor from her past.

Maybe, just maybe, some things were allowed to remain hidden, lost and forgotten, covered in dust and cobwebs where they belonged.

Somehow, this strange, nearly morbid thought brought a soft sigh to Ilse's lips. She glanced at the sealed interrogation room door, listening to the muffled, but indeterminable sound of voices from within.

"Did they run the bowie knife yet?" she said, quietly.

Sawyer rubbed at his jaw, giving her a long look. Again, it seemed, perhaps, like the sort of question he ought not answer to a civilian. But again, likely against protocol, he just shook his head. "Not yet. Looks like there might be blood on it though."

Ilse felt a little shiver of relief. She could feel the excitement at the prospect of returning home, of telling Samantha the good news.

The bastard was behind bars. She was safe.

Ilse winced, though, remembering her promise. She'd told Sam she'd be back within ten minutes. She'd been gone for more than an hour, now. Samantha was probably terrified. Ilse swallowed, feeling a sudden jolt of urgency to get back and calm her client.

"Guy had a record," Sawyer continued, expressionless, watching her like an owl perched on a branch. "Violence against women. Sexual misconduct. Been escalating in recent years." Sawyer gave her a long look and swallowed. He opened his mouth, but Ilse beat him to it.

"I know," she said, wincing. "Stupid."

This time, she was sure he grinned. He turned, though, hiding the expression and nodding once. He began to walk away, and Ilse fell into step next to the agent as they both moved toward the sliding glass doors of the precinct.

"So this is over," Ilse said, softly and urgently, Samantha still on her mind. "Are they going to ask him about the other victims back at the shack?"

"Yup."

"How about the two victims found on the side of the road?"

"Mhmm."

"Good… That's good." Ilse winced. "I hate to think what he might have done with them… I'd been thinking he'd left Samantha alive just to torment her. But what if… what if he left her alive to… to do things?" She shivered and broke off the sentence, glancing to the side and clenching a fist against her knee. Her sweatshirt felt old and worn now, and she wanted nothing more than to placate Samantha and take a long, steamy shower. Maybe two, and then change into something clean. Then sleep for days.

Sawyer glanced back, hands jutting in his jeans pockets, and he shrugged once. "Thanks, Doc." Then, without so much as a goodbye, he turned and slunk off toward the office space in the back of the precinct.

Ilse watched him go, feeling a frown of curiosity crease her features. A strange man, Sawyer. But good at his job. Dependable, too, it seemed. She still wasn't quite sure what had gotten into her, to use herself as bait, texting the agent as if she'd known he would show up.

What if Sawyer had ignored the text?

What if he'd been slow?

Despite his gruff nature, he seemed an odd combination of reserved and emotionally stunted, combined with protective and diligent. A man of instinct and action.

It was Ilse's turn to smile once, nodding in approval and then turning toward the doors to the precinct. Now, she could go home, take that shower, and tell Samantha the good news.

It was all over.

CHAPTER TWENTY FIVE

The lock clicked behind Ilse. This time, she double-checked, but didn't triple-check. Incremental progress—small baby steps instead of concrete shoes. She moved away from the door with a sigh, grateful to be back home. As she moved in the dark, she glanced toward the couch.

Two wide eyes stared out from beneath a comforter and a couple of sheets.

"Hello?" came Samantha's voice. "Who is that!"

"It's me," said Ilse. "Dr. Beck. It's just me. I'm so sorry I'm late. But I have good news."

There was a pause, and the eyes on the couch flashed. A shadow moved, one of the sheets falling off the form as a hand pulled on the chain of a small lamp. The small space illuminated, the light reflecting off the glass door that led to the patio.

Samantha had the comforter up to her chin, her legs now pulled up against her, creating a bump in the middle where it looked like she'd wrapped her arms around her knees, hugging them to her body. She rocked back and forth a bit, a soothing, soft motion.

"Good news?" Samantha said, quietly. "Where were you?"

"I got sidetracked," Ilse said, wincing. "Sorry. But yeah, really good news. They caught the guy."

Samantha stared.

"I was there, I saw him." She paused, then frowned. "Aaaand… I forgot the pizza. Damn it. Sorry."

"I'm not hungry. They—they caught him?"

Ilse bobbed her head. "Was some creep, perving up and down the mountain roads, looking for victims. He's with the police right now. He's done."

Samantha let out a desperate, soft little cry. Her eyes seemed bright in the lamplight, shimmering with a film of mist. "What does he look like?" she said, her voice hoarse, barely even a croak.

At this, Ilse felt a flash of pity. She softly said, "It isn't the same guy from when you were a kid, Sam. I'm so sorry. It's someone else. Just a creep. Young guy. In his twenties. He had a record and everything."

"Oh…" Sam said, softly. Her hands seemed to tighten around her legs.

"You can go home if you'd like. Or stay, either way. If you want, I could drive you."

Samantha shifted some more, the thick bandages along her neck standing out over the collar of her borrowed pajamas. "I… it wasn't him?"

"No, too young. I'm sorry, Sam. You're safe now. He's no longer going to hurt you. No one is. You're safe."

"You're sure? Did he have an older guy he was working with? Maybe… maybe someone with a red truck?" She spoke hopefully, a soft little desperate lilt to her tone.

Ilse shook her head. "No, sorry. Just the one guy. It's not him. You're safe now, Sam."

"Can—can I stay here? Just for the night?"

"Of course." Even as she said it, Ilse could feel another jolt of sympathy. She watched where Sam hunched, trembling, arms wrapped around her legs. She felt a flicker of regret that Sam's old abductor hadn't been caught. He was still out there, still a source of fear.

And Sam was here, still awake, still paranoid. She didn't look relieved at the news, though. If anything, she seemed even more nervous than at the start of the night. She was worrying at her lip, gnawing so hard that it looked like she might draw blood if she wasn't careful.

Ilse felt a flash of frustration. Not at Sam. But at the memories. At the trauma so deeply set that she was still stuck, still terrified.

"What if it's not the right guy?" Sam said, quietly. "Are they sure? How sure? It's not the right guy, Dr. Beck! It's not! Someone's out there, trying to find *me.* They're after *me.* I know it! I know it, Dr. Beck!"

Ilse hurried over, her feet padding against the floorboards. She reached the couch, and then, with gentle, easy motions she settled on the couch, reaching out and patting the blanket next to Sam's foot, careful not to actually make physical contact. One had to be delicate in such situations. Touch was a stress-regulator in development, but with trauma, the effect could be reversed into something more damaging.

"It's the right guy, Sam," Ilse said. "You're safe now."

"I don't know, Dr. Beck… I don't know. I can… I can feel it. Do you know what I mean? I can feel it."

Ilse's own memories flashed. In her mind's eye she glimpsed two glaring, mismatched eyes. She did know what Sam meant. Knew it all too well, too deeply. She shivered and shook her head. Sam's trauma was so deep-set, so ingrained in her identity that she might never move past it. She would always think her tormentor was still out there. She would always be looking over her shoulder…

Unless Ilse did something about it.

Ilse felt iron behind her words now as she spoke, one hand still resting on the comforter, near Samantha's trembling foot beneath the blanket. "I'm going to help you, Samantha," Ilse said. "I swear it. You have my word. I'm going to help."

"Help?" Sam said the word with a rasping croak, as if she couldn't quite believe it. Her eyes fluttered, half closed. Clearly, she was exhausted. "That'd be nice," Sam murmured, her voice growing more faint.

"I promise," Ilse said, nodding. The promise wasn't so much for Sam as it was for Ilse herself. She meant it.

Sam needed help, and Ilse was determined to give it. No matter how long it took.

"Dr. Beck," Sam said, quietly. "Is it—is it okay if I leave the light on? Just for a bit."

"That's fine, Sam. You should get some rest. The doors are locked. The killer is behind bars. You're safe. I promise you."

"Thanks."

Ilse smiled at Samantha, but the gesture didn't quite come from her heart. Mostly, she only felt grief and sadness. Sometimes old wounds went so deep they caused pain decades later. Crippling, isolating pain.

It wasn't fair.

But Ilse was going to help. At least she knew that much. She patted the blanket, still not quite making contact with Sam's foot, and then moved slowly, cautiously toward her bedroom. First a shower, then another… Then some fresh clothes.

She sighed, feeling a shiver of delight. Then, mercifully, she'd finally be able to get some sleep.

***

As much as she wanted to, Ilse found it difficult to fall asleep. Her hair was damp, following the long, half-hour shower. It was nice to feel clean for the first time in two days. She had changed into another sweatshirt with sweatpants. Now, as she lay in her bed, staring up at the motionless fan on the ceiling, she could feel her heart flutter in her chest.

The darkness was oppressive, and it came with friends.

Ilse gritted her teeth, wincing against the deluge of memories playing across her flitting subconscious. Every time her mind seemed to try and dip into rest, the memories would return, like burglars pouncing at the opportunity. Ilse's fists clenched, one hand bunched and caught up in the covers. The house seemed smaller than she remembered, her bedroom tiny.

She shifted a bit, and felt something lumpy brush her cheek. Were those feathers?

She yelped, and twisted sharply.

But it was just her pillow, pressed up next to her face. Trembling, she pushed at the pillow, her fingers probing, just to make sure it was only bedding.

She could remember, could still feel the warmth of the dead pigeon, could still hear the crack of its bones—the pain in her finger. Could still smell her father's stale and warm breath against her cheek. Could still hear his voice grating and rasping in her ear.

She reached up in the dark, embraced by the bed, her fingers probing at her ear, gently touching against the missing lobe on the right side; with the same fingers she traced that horrible scar, trailing down to her chin.

She couldn't sleep. Not now, not after the last couple of days.

"Dammit," Ilse murmured.

She tried to shift the other direction, pulling the comforter up to her ear. She tried turning the pillow on its cooler side. But try as she might, she couldn't rest. Unwanted, horrible memories played like movies inside her eyelids.

She glanced toward the door to the bathroom, wondering if she still had some sleeping pills in the medicine cabinet.

Then, while trying to summon the energy to hop out of bed and retrieve the pills, there came a quiet tapping sound against the door.

Two quick knocks.

Ilse froze. The sound was a strange one, echoing in her room. Someone was knocking on the wooden door… But another sound was conjured in her mind. More a memory. She remembered the basement stairs back in Germany. Remembered the same tapping sound—footsteps against the floorboards above, a warning that her father was coming. She could remember the way her siblings, her brothers and sisters in the dark, had writhed and hidden behind the couch or moved to their sleeping bags. Others had grabbed the sparse books they'd been allowed, pretending to be deep in study.

Ilse snapped back to the present, breathing in shallow puffs and staring at her door.

"Yes?" Ilse called out.

"Dr. Beck?" came Samantha's trembling voice. "I'm sorry, Dr. Beck. I, I—"

"Is everything all right?" Ilse said, strangely grateful to have someone else's fears to worry about for a moment.

"I can't sleep."

You and me both, Ilse thought. Out loud, she said, "Did you try turning off the lamp?"

"It's too scary out there. I don't like being on my own. I-I can still feel them," Samantha whispered. "The bodies in that basement. How they brushed against me. I can still feel them."

Ilse winced, remembering the scene, the strange, gruesome smiley face created from corpses. Remembering where they had found Samantha, buried among the dead, left to bleed out in the pitch-black. She supposed she couldn't blame her. "Do you think it would be better if—"

"Can I sleep in there?"

Ilse frowned. "I can take the couch if that would make it—"

"No! I don't want to be alone."

Then the door handle turned, and the door creaked slowly, with a quiet grating sound.

Everything remained plunged in darkness, and Ilse realized the hallway light was off, and all she could make out was Samantha's silhouette against the doorway.

"I won't bother you," Sam whispered, desperately. "I promise. I just can't be alone." She stepped into the room.

Ilse frowned. "I don't know if that's—"

Before she could complete the sentence, the door clicked shut. Ilse listened to the sound of padding feet against the floor, and she glimpsed Samantha's shadow caught by the faintest of lights through the shuttered curtains over the window. She watched as the woman then circled the bed, moving over toward the empty side of the queen-sized mattress.

"I can remember now," Sam whispered.

Ilse winced, wondering exactly how to extricate herself from this uncomfortable situation. "It's fine," she tried again, "you can take the bed. I'll go in the other room."

"Please," Samantha said, desperately. "Don't leave me. Please—please don't."

Ilse was now propped up on one elbow, and she felt a jolt of discomfort as Samantha slid into the bed next to her, pulling near.

For a moment, Ilse just sat there resting on one elbow, frowning to herself. She tried to turn, to face the other direction, if only for a little bit of privacy. Inwardly, she cycled through what she might be able to do. Could she just tell Samantha to leave? Did she really want to offend the woman like that? If she got up and left to the other room, would Samantha be upset? She was clearly in a very fragile place. Still, this was extremely odd. Having a client in her house after hours was one thing. Sharing a bedroom, no less a bed, though…

"I can remember," Samantha whispered, her voice close to Ilse's ear. "I remember more now. So much more."

Ilse remained stiff, not quite leaving yet, but not relaxing either.

"I remember how he would come home. You could hear his footsteps on the floorboards above."

Ilse frowned as Samantha spoke; it was as if her client's words were conjuring thoughts from deep in Ilse's own mind. She heard the creak of the floorboards, could see the light beneath the door in her memories.

"…then the light would turn on beneath the door," Sam continued. "The others were down there, and they would shiver and shake. We were all so scared."

"What do you mean?" Ilse said, her voice dry all of a sudden.

"I mean," Samantha murmured, her voice echoing in the still, dark bedroom, "he wasn't a nice man. I remember how he killed that pigeon. Don't you?"

A shiver pawed up Ilse's spine, and she went as still as ice. She heard the *crunch* in her memories, could feel her sprained finger, could feel the blood beneath her hands. She swallowed.

"What did you say?"

Ilse felt a small hand rest on her shoulder, felt Samantha wrap her arms around her, hugging her from behind, her body warm.

"We have the same memory," Samantha continued. "How couldn't we? We are sisters, after all."

CHAPTER TWENTY SIX

Ilse froze in terror, a wave of panic rushing through her like water surging through a burst dam. It all came flooding back. Her *sister.* One of many Ilse had left behind when she'd escaped.

Ilse, panicking, writhed and struggled to break free—but Samantha held her tight.

"Let me go!" Ilse said, her voice uncontrolled, desperate and high-pitched. "Get off me! Let me go!"

But Samantha ignored her, whispering still, her voice hissing in Ilse's ear. "He loved those scissors. He liked the sound they made when they hurt us. He enjoyed doing horrible things. You remember. Do you remember? I'm so sorry that he did that to you. Your ear. You had such beautiful little ears."

Ilse could feel the ice in her chest now. Fear and confusion prickled across her. She swallowed, but the lump lodged in her throat. She tried to twist, but could feel Sam's arms now wrapping tighter around her shoulders, holding her in place. Not so much a hug anymore, but a restraining embrace.

"I don't think we should have gone through that. That was terrible, wasn't it, Hilda? We had a terrible father. Didn't we, sister? I wish we hadn't. I really do. Please, no, stop struggling. I'm here. Stop it, stop it!" Samantha screamed this last phrase. Her voice was no longer trembling, no longer shaking. Her voice was no longer desperate or pitiable. It was a loud, bellowing, furious tone. A voice of command and power.

It reverberated, echoing in Ilse's ears. The arms that had seemed soft, comforting, embracing at first were now like iron cords wrapped against Ilse's shoulders.

"Get off me!" Ilse yelled, kicking now, but the blankets tangled her legs, wrapping around them like a constrictor and helping to hold her fast.

"He shouldn't have done that. We shouldn't have suffered like that. It wasn't right. It wasn't very fun."

And then Ilse felt Samantha's hand moving up her shoulder, moving up to her lips. She could smell something strong. A rag? Some strange odor. Was that chloroform?

"Get off!"

Ilse tried to knock back with her head, but she only hit a pillow. She tried to flail, but Samantha was surprisingly strong.

Samantha was giggling now, all signs of the trembling tone vanished. "There, there, baby sister. Rock-a-bye baby. Smile, smile. It's all going to be okay. Remember, *you* said that. You're the one who promised. You should be careful what you promise."

Ilse could feel her eyes drooping, the scent of chemicals against her nose; her eyes stinging. She tried to struggle, but her hands were going limp. She felt Samantha behind her, wrapping her arms tight. The woman who claimed to be her sister leaned in. She felt soft lips against her cheek.

Samantha kissed her gently, cooing in her ear. "There, there. It's all going to be okay, baby sister. It's all going to be just fine. I promise. I *really* promise." Her words were biting, acerbic.

All fight had fled Ilse's limbs. She couldn't move, couldn't shout, couldn't do anything but slowly, bathed in terror and chemicals, drift off into a dark embrace.

CHAPTER TWENTY SEVEN

Ilse's eyes felt weighted with lead. She couldn't quite blink at first, as her consciousness returned in gentle pulses. It started in her chest as a prickle, then along her arms and her back. Then her cheeks itched, and finally, her eyelids, under the peculiar weight of chemical interference, began to flutter. As her eyes opened, the horror that had confronted her before falling unconscious returned to her memory.

She went stiff, even as her vision adjusted.

All around her, glass. Glass windows, glass walls. A couch, and a sofa, and a desk chair near a bookcase. They were in the patio office. Where she had tried to help Samantha.

A fake name, no doubt.

Ilse coughed, groaning as she strained, trying to sit forward. She was on the couch, in the middle seat, pressed against the cushions, as if swallowed by comfort. She tried to stand up, to push off, her instincts taking over, but the moment she did, her shoulders ached, and she realized her arms were bound behind her, useless and wedged against the couch.

"Help…" she managed to gasp out, the word coming strangled from her lips. But the sound came muffled, and she realized a gag was wrapped over her mouth. "Help," she tried again, louder, but the word was caught by the fabric.

Now, panic was returning, settling as a prickle from her head to her toes. At least her legs weren't bound. Her wrists chafed, and she tried to twist them behind her back to loosen them, but this only elicited a groan from her gagged mouth. She exhaled through her nose slowly.

As her eyes adjusted once more, and the chemical persuasion wore off, Ilse's gaze adjusted and she found herself focusing on the single silhouette stalking back and forth, outlined against the glass facing the lake. It was night; far too dark to see much beyond the first row of trees. The porch itself didn't have much in the way of illumination, save a single light in the center of the ceiling, which could be turned on with the chain, though it was dim currently. The only illumination came from the moon above, allowed, on the rare occasion, to peek through the usually overcast skies.

"Well, isn't this a predicament," came Samantha's cheerful voice.

The stalking silhouette came to a halt, illuminated by the glimmer and glow of the moon behind her, past the trees and over the lake.

Ilse tried to respond, but what was the use? The sounds wouldn't come past the makeshift gag.

"Little Hilda Mueller," said Samantha in a singsong voice. Gone was the trembling in her tone. Gone were the frightened glances from side to side; gone was the terror in every furtive gesture. Now, there was something cocky, amused about the way she was watching Ilse. Her head was tilted.

Samantha's hair was no longer blonde. Now, she had dark hair the exact same color as Ilse's. A blonde wig lay discarded on the ground by Samantha's foot. On top of the wig, a small, blue plastic can of pepper spray. The same can from Ilse's key chain. Samantha must have nabbed it when Ilse wasn't looking. But why?

The answer, though, seemed horribly obvious.

To disarm her. To remove all forms of self-defense before… Before what?

"I don't understand," Ilse tried, her voice shaking. Already she was piecing things together, and the puzzles forming in her mind didn't end in a pretty picture. She could feel shivers speeding along her spine. Could feel her heart quickening, her mouth dry as if she had been sucking on cotton swabs.

"There we go," said Samantha in that singsong way. "There we go, I can see it in your eyes, little sister. Don't you remember me? I thought for sure when I first saw you it might click. I knew you the moment my eyes met yours. But I don't think you recognized me. How about now?"

She turned, one way and then the other, like a fashion model walking the catwalk, trying to display her features. She gave a comical little shake of her head, then her chest, before tossing her hair and fluffing it with one hand. She fluttered her eyelashes, the motion barely visible in the dim lights.

"Please…" Ilse tried to say, her voice still heavily muffled. She exhaled through her nose again. She needed her lips. Needed to speak. It was the only real tool she had. She was unarmed, bound, trapped. She knew she had spent time in that basement, back in the Black Forest in Germany, with others. Brothers and sisters she had called them. Had they been biological siblings? Stepsiblings? Strangers who she had bonded with? She couldn't quite remember. For Ilse it wasn't play acting, nor was it pretend. So many of her memories had been washed away like sand castles on the shore, hit with a tidal wave. So many of the things she wished she could recall, and even more of the things she was grateful she couldn't, were hidden, submerged beneath the murky thoughts of her subconscious.

Regardless, now it seemed clear enough. Samantha wasn't a client at all. She'd been lying, pretending. She had been in that basement in Germany, too. The postcards, of course, had been sent by her. But beyond that, Ilse wasn't sure how deep it went.

Still, she knew she was in danger… terrible danger. She shuddered, picturing the bodies strewn across the floor of the basement in that shack. She needed her words, needed her voice. But how could she get Samantha to remove the gag? She didn't even know who Samantha was anymore. She'd been so very, very wrong. About everything. About the paranoia. About the killer. Was there even a killer?

The thought alone sent a shiver up Ilse's spine.

There was a killer because there were corpses. But now, she realized with a start, nothing Samantha had told her could be trusted.

She couldn't piece it all together. Not like this, not struggling with her thoughts, as the chemical weight of the chloroform lifted. One thing at a time. She needed to be able to speak. If she wanted to survive, to make it another ten minutes, she knew she needed the ability to talk.

And so she began to speak quietly. She leaned back instead of forward, and kept her expression very serious and solemn as she took on the tone of a chiding mother, trying to correct her errant daughter. The words, of course, were muffled and gibberish. It wasn't about what she was saying, just the tone she was saying it in. Her wrists still ached behind her. Her hands throbbed with pain.

"What did you say?" Samantha taunted. She tapped her ear. "I can't quite hear you, little sister."

Instead of rising to the bait, or showing any more fear, though, Ilse kept her expression calm, placid. She kept her shoulders squared, her chin high, leaning back again, everything in her posture suggesting she was actually in control. It was the posture of a businessperson during a job interview. The posture of a banker, refusing to approve a loan. The posture of a teacher ready to reprimand a child. The posture of a mother facing her daughter. Nonverbal cues, placid expression, all of it designed to irritate, but also to attract attention.

Ilse spoke again, this time shifting her head side to side, punctuating the nonsense gibberish she was muttering beneath her breath with a shake of her head and a delicate little sigh. No fear in her eyes. No fear in her posture.

Samantha was clearly a narcissist. Multiple personality disorder, perhaps. Though now, Ilse didn't think so. Samantha was all too aware of what she had been doing while blubbering and carrying on. No, not multiple personality disorder. Antisocial personality disorder with psychopathic tendencies. And psychopaths with social disorders liked control above all. They considered themselves special, and liked to consider themselves powerful. If they felt that power threatened, they would inflict pain. In their minds, control and pain were often correlated. Especially when there was trauma in the past.

And so Ilse knew the blow was coming before it even started. She knew Samantha would strike her. And she knew, exactly then, what her response would have to be. She needed the gag off.

Samantha lashed out, just as Ilse knew she would. Her fist colliding with her purported sister's cheek. Expecting it, Ilse leaned the other way and received a glancing blow. It hurt, but not too badly. Instead of reacting to the punch, though, which would have been conceding control, in a strange, roundabout sort of way, she made a clicking sound accompanied by a disapproving little shake of her head. Again, designed to infuriate, to drain the control from the situation. It was all smoke and mirrors. Samantha was clearly in control. Ilse was bound, gagged. She had no cards left to play.

But antisocial personality disorder, mixed with narcissistic tendencies, especially with someone who clearly had a violent temper, while frightening, could also be exploited. Killers were not self-controlled individuals. They lacked self-control at their very core. They directed it toward a single outlet, often enough. And many of them, to the surprise of most of the public, could delay gratification, blending in like a chameleon.

But once they removed their masks, it was like an actor stepping center stage, basking in the limelight.

And in so doing, they felt their afforded and required response would be one of awe and fear. But if a narcissist wasn't greeted with the emotion they expected, it could gnaw at the very thing they guarded most about themselves. Their ego. Their control.

But this wasn't enough. Simply shaking her head, leaning back, posturing herself wouldn't do anything. Ilse also needed the gag removed. Which was why she was speaking. Not in an obnoxious, challenging sort of way. That would've only seen her beaten. Pain was an easy enough tool. Everyone caved under it eventually to varying degrees.

This time, she inflected her voice. Again, through the gag, it was nearly impossible to voice words. She was even running out of breath now, feeling her throat rattle as she spoke. But she tilted the words toward the end of the sentence up, now, inflecting them as questions, and tilting her chin, as if waiting for a response.

"What?" Samantha demanded.

Ilse just repeated the gesture, the motion, and the intonation, as if it were the most natural thing in the world. Even though, sitting bound and gagged, the fear, the panic, and, oddly, the silliness of it all was wearing thin.

"What?" Samantha demanded, growling. She reached out and yanked the gag down.

One step forward. Ilse could talk now.

Ilse grabbed the nearest question she could, hoping that by engaging, the gag wouldn't be returned to its place. She breathed slowly as she did, refusing to display any sort of distress.

"What are you doing this for?" Ilse said.

"Really, little sister? I thought you were supposed to be some big bad head shrink. Imagine my surprise, just a year ago, when I read a magazine—at an airport no less. And there you were, page thirty-three, standing next to a man with a big white beard. I recognized you instantly, Hilda. But the name; that I didn't recognize. Ilse Beck. Strange," Samantha said, conversationally, shifting again. "You changed your name. You've changed your accent too. No one could even tell you're from Germany, not if they didn't know you from before."

Ilse swallowed, trying to track. "I don't understand. *Who* are you?"

This, clearly, was the wrong question. Samantha's eyes narrowed beneath her dark fringe, fury etching across her features. "Seriously? You don't remember me? You don't remember your own sister, Hilda?"

Ilse strained, her memory fluttering back. She winced, shaking her head, trying to focus. But there were so many swirling thoughts and old recollections. So many buried secrets and forgotten horrors.

"I wish I did. I really do. Is your name Samantha?"

"Heidi Mueller." She said it with a roll of the *R*, flourishing the words as if presenting a gift. Again, it was clear she expected a reaction. But if Ilse was supposed to remember that name, she simply couldn't.

"You were back in Germany with me? In," her voice trembled, "in that basement?"

Heidi Mueller was frowning even more deeply now. She seemed put off by Ilse's reactions. "Twenty years ago now. But yes, I was there. There were seven of us. Don't you remember, Hilda? Please say you remember *something.* I know you do. I hid my accent too. You're not the only clever one. But you've hidden your memories, it seems. Not me—I remember everything."

Ilse winced, trying to think back, to distract her attacker another moment longer. Desperately, she struggled to recollect. But her thoughts returned to a blank. It was like trying to study a painting with her eyes closed or trying to watch a movie through a gray sheet.

"I don't remember nearly anything from back then," Ilse murmured softly. "I remember it was horrible. I remember *him.*"

Heidi sneered now, her face twisting into an expression of rage. "We all remember him. But you should remember *me*. You promised you'd come back for me. Or did you forget that part too? Conveniently forgot it, didn't you? For three weeks we waited. Three weeks we suffered while you took your jolly old time to send help. That *wasn't* the plan!"

Heidi's voice was now increasing in anger. A simmering, slow-burning rage shone behind her eyes now, even in the dark gloom of the glass patio.

"I don't remember," Ilse murmured. Even as she said it, a jolt of guilt panged in her chest. She didn't remember making a plan. Three weeks? What did Heidi mean by three weeks? Ilse had long felt guilt at leaving the others back in that basement. She didn't recall their names or their faces. She didn't recall much. But she did know there had been others down there. She didn't know how she had managed to escape. She hadn't known what had happened to the others. She couldn't even recollect how she had escaped. Vaguely, she thought of a glass window. She remembered the sound of shattering. Screaming, the stomping of feet. She remembered hands at her back, pushing, pushing. A whispered, strained voice, yelling, "Go!"

Sensations and feelings and words. But that was it. She couldn't remember much more.

"You should've come back like you promised, little sister. Not just send proxy help weeks later. Not so delayed. The police said you were half-starved when they found you on the side of the road. Having survived the forest. But you were slow, so very slow. When they found us," Heidi said, swallowing, "it was late. It got horrible after you escaped. He killed two of our brothers. Hans and Dietrich. He beat them to death. He thought they were the ones who helped you!"

Ilse winced, reeling, desperate, the gag tickling her chin. Her hands strained in pain, wedged against the couch behind her. What was Samantha—no—*Heidi* talking about? Police? Three weeks? Had Ilse managed to call for help? How come she didn't remember any of it? Not a whiff of a scent. Nothing. All of it gone, eaten up by a forgetful, traumatized mind.

She tried to twist, to glance over her shoulder, wondering if a car might pass by the forest road, wondering at the trees shaking and whistling with the wind, occasionally discarding an unwanted leaf, and watching as it fluttered, twisting and spinning to the ground to join the carpet of detritus.

Night still stretched across the sky, still peeked through the windows, still carpeted the trees, and the forest and the lake and everything it touched, washing it with shadow.

And the two of them were alone.

One of them remembering the horrors back in that little house, in that basement. The other stuck, lost in thought, memories fleeting. One of them full of rage. The other trembling with fear.

"Police? The police found you? At the house? Father? Was—what happened?"

Heidi stared at Ilse hard, as if trying to decide if she were playing pretend. Her eyes narrowed, though, and she sneered. "Yes… Police. Three weeks after you promised. Three weeks of horrors later. Two deaths later. Father is in prison, little Hilda. Are you telling me you don't even remember that? They put that strange-eyed bastard behind bars, where I couldn't reach him." She snarled, spittle flying from bared teeth like some wounded wolf. "But he might be safe in jail… They never found the extent of what he'd done. You, on the other hand. My little sister. The one who waited three weeks to get help. Wandered stupid around a forest, stumbling into trees and over roots and eating your own shit, no doubt. You're the one who caused those three weeks of hell! You should have stuck to the plan! You *never* came back!" Heidi screamed so loudly, one of the windows shuddered. She kicked at the blonde wig, sending it shooting toward Ilse's couch. The pepper spray rolled under the furniture, out of sight. Another little tinge of hope vanishing.

Ilse squeaked, "I don't know anything about a plan! I don't

remember any of it!"

Heidi drew nearer, her presence looming, her shadow like the essence of some ghoul. "You don't remember me helping you? The way I broke that window? You couldn't even reach it. You were so small! You never came back for us, Hilda! You never returned!"

Ilse winced. Again, she remembered the sound of shattering glass. Again she could remember the feeling of fingers at her back, pushing her, encouraging words launched after her, before the torrential sound of screaming and rage. And then… then what?

Rapid footfalls of bare feet against dusty ground. Cold pine needles. Pain. Ricocheting off a tree. Gasping, gasping. Wincing against the sunlight. Stumbling, desperately, racing through the forest, away, away. A single glance back. Shattered glass in the window. Bars that had been slowly whittled away. With knives? No, it hadn't been knives. A rope? She seemed to remember a length of rope. They had hidden it not *behind* the couch, but in it. Resting it against the wooden brace through the fabric. Their father had even found the cut portion of the couch.

He had thought they'd been negligent. He had beaten one of them for it. Ilse couldn't remember who. She couldn't remember their faces. Two of them dead because of her escape? She didn't even remember those names. She hoped perhaps by hearing it would have conjured a thought, an image of a face—anything! But all it brought was guilt. More guilt to go along with the heaping shame she always felt. Guilt she'd felt since she'd been a teenager. Guilt she'd felt ever since she'd left Germany to escape to America. Guilt she'd felt while trained by Dr. Mitchell. Guilt while auditing those classes. Guilt while going through college, getting her advanced degrees, starting her own practice. Guilt she'd felt every day, unless she forced her mind to flit away. Unless she buried those memories. Because she didn't have the full picture. She only knew the horrors.

And sometimes, when memories were lost, it was possible to pretend things had never happened to begin with. It was easier that way.

But now, the wraith in the mirror, the mist in the graveyard, the forgotten thing was in front of her, a shadow in the glass. An omen from her past. A demon in her consciousness. And she felt nearly certain it was about to try and kill her.

CHAPTER TWENTY EIGHT

Ilse's voice shook as she tried to speak past her own whirring thoughts. "I should've come back for you. I didn't remember. I-I don't know why it took me three weeks to get the police. I don't even think—so much time had passed. I didn't even know you'd been freed by the police. I didn't know Dad was in prison!" Even as she said it, Ilse felt a shuddering little pulse of relief.

Just as quickly as the rage had come, Samantha buried it with a fake smile. She tossed her hair again and gave a little shake of her head. "I'm not there anymore, am I? Obviously. It cost me pain. But he never found out I was the one who helped you. Besides, he liked hurting us regardless. It wasn't like too much could change. We did get starved for nearly three weeks. He didn't let us out in the yard for that month. And he spent weeks looking for you. Most of us didn't think you'd make it far, anyway. But we'd counted on you… Hoped on you. All you had to do was go straight to the police. You were the only one who could fit through that window. Small as you were. You're still pretty small, aren't you?"

Ilse swallowed. She wasn't sure how to react to the switch in tone and demeanor. From rageful and furious, to cavalier and carefree. Playacting. A pretense. Just another way to regain control. But Ilse couldn't show that she knew it. One of the worst ways to rile someone like this was to call them out on their script.

So instead, Ilse changed the subject, her voice shaking. "You saw me in a magazine?"

"A college magazine, if I remember. Purely an accident I even found it. I overhead someone saying there was an article with research on serial killer survivors. There was a photo of a man named Dr. Donovan Mitchell."

Ilse winced now, remembering the article in question. It had been for the university's newspaper. She hadn't even meant to be in that photo. She'd been behind Dr. Mitchell, working on her computer, when the photographer had taken the shot.

"You recognized me? From that?"

"I've always had a good eye for faces. Especially faces that I spent years with, trapped, without being able to see anyone else."

Ilse thought of the postcard of the Black Forest. The postcard of that small little town. Heidi had been taunting her, teasing.

Ilse struggled to make sense. "I don't understand. You mentioned a barn… a red truck…"

"Bullshit. Made it all up." Samantha grinned now, nodding. And for the first time, Ilse's widening eyes weren't an act.

The look of surprise clearly pleased Samantha, and she clicked her tongue. "You know what I'm going to do for you, little sister. Instead of making you fish, and look, and trouble that pretty little head of yours, how about I help you out here. I'll *tell* you what's eating at you. See, I had to throw you off. I couldn't tell you that I was harmed in Germany. I couldn't tell you about the basement. You'd know it was me. Though, I guess you wouldn't. You still don't seem to remember me. Which is really quite hurtful."

Heidi shook her head in mock severity. Wagging a finger, she said, "I needed to get close. And so I scheduled my first meeting with Dr. Mitchell. Nice guy that. Good eyes. Of course, I didn't give him a thing. Closed down immediately. Hinting, quite obviously, I might add, that I could only speak to a woman. I figured he'd know who you were. Since he was in that picture too. It didn't take long for him to refer me to you. First name on the list he gave." Heidi grinned now, her teeth forming a crescent moon in the dark.

She began to stalk back and forth again, giving a little hop skip every couple of steps, as if she were a child at play.

"Why?" Ilse said, swallowing deeply. "I don't understand. Why do any of that?"

"Ah. I see how it might be confusing. Because, little sister. I wanted to fucking slit your throat."

Heidi said it jokingly, playful. Skipping once more and landing with a little *thump*, facing the glass and looking in the direction of the lake.

Ilse went stiff. "Because I didn't come back for you?"

"Yes. Obviously. I'm not sure I've been able to emphasize to you, little sister, just how much I hate your guts. You left me down there. For three long weeks. He did some real nasty things to me, I can tell you. You're lucky you hadn't hit puberty yet… Tut, tut. I don't want to trouble you, little sister." Heidi gave a whistle and made a whirling motion near her head. "Real tough times, let me tell you. I mean like, wow. Hellish. Truly, hellish. And once you escaped, Dad tripled everything. He just went *off* on us! Hard! I'm lucky he didn't kill me too, though it was a close thing. Because of *you* not sticking to the plan."

"I'm so sorry. If I'd remembered. If I knew—"

"All right, shut up. I don't want to hear your pity party. *If I'd remembered. If I knew.*" Heidi began to hyperventilate, her eyes wide, her lip trembling. A single tear traced down the inside of her cheek all of a sudden. "I just need help. Please, he's after me." Just as quickly as she adopted the mask, she let it slip again, smiling, wiping away the tear and winking. "It was so easy. You shrinks think you're so smart. All your degrees and training. Famous Ilse Beck, therapist and psychologist, or whatever it is you call yourself. It's all shit. You can't even see through the easiest con I've ever done. Granted, I have had some practice. It took a little to get across the border; I've been living in California, actually. For about five years now. It was a pretty good life. Well, at least as good as you can get. Got some trouble with the cops down there. You know how it is."

"I don't know how it is."

"No, I guess you wouldn't. Because, if we both remember, you got out. And I was left stuck there to fester. Because you lied. And you *never* came back." She pointed both fingers at Ilse now, accusingly.

"I don't know what else to say besides I'm sorry. Three weeks is a long time. But we'd been down there for years. And I didn't even remember who or where to come back to!"

"Yes, but we all knew how *he* would react when one of us escaped. He told us what he'd do! He warned us! He drew pictures, demonstrated. You knew, and you still didn't stick to the bloody plan!" Heidi screamed. "I'm not looking for an *apology*, little sister. I'm going to kill you. Horribly. I'm still trying to think of how to do it. There's got to be some poetic way. I think they'll probably write a book about us one day. Maybe I'll write it, on the run or something."

Ilse fingers were numb. Her lips trembled, but she forced herself to stay calm as best she could. "I understand that you're angry." Ilse could feel the trickle of fear along her back. She could feel the weight of her sister's words latching on like burrs. She couldn't show fear, not yet. She tried to strain, tried to move her hands.

Heidi tapped a finger to her lips. "Do you remember how we passed notes to each other in the basement? When we weren't allowed to talk? When he threatened to cut out your tongue if you spoke again? Do you remember that?"

"Notes?" Ilse said, her voice hoarse.

"Yes, notes. Like these." Heidi pulled out a small pile of sticky notes from her pocket. "We used to pass them back and forth between our sleeping bags. I can even remember how you used to giggle, when I would do those cartoon smiley faces. I was just trying to make you laugh. It was the only sound of joy I ever remembered. I miss that."

Heidi trailed off for a moment, staring out the window, lost in thought it seemed.

Ilse took that moment to desperately try to twist her wrists. But she was unarmed. There were no weapons. She glanced at the desk. There, in the cup holder, next to a pen, was a pair of scissors. How could she reach them though? She slid, ever so subtly, an inch to the right. Her legs weren't bound, mercifully. She needed to reach the scissors. A desperate goal. But what else could she do?

"See, little sister," Heidi said, softly. "There was no killer. I just needed to raise the stakes, to get you invested and involved. To get you alone. To get you to think I was in danger. It's really funny how people with weak consciences will put themselves in harm's way for another, to assuage their own guilt. And so I let you do that. And you did do it. You did it to yourself. Because you wanted to be my savior; you thought little Samantha Wright was in danger. And so you tried to protect me; it's really quite admirable. A couple of decades too late, of course. But admirable."

Another surreptitious inch to the right. More stalling. Just a bit longer. "Those women. The ones that were killed. Did you—were you the one who—did you—" Ilse tried to keep the horror from her voice.

"Duh. I killed them. You really have to work at getting to the point, sister. For those first two sessions, I have to tell you, I wanted to yawn a couple of times. But then again, I knew I needed you to play that sympathy card. I needed you on my side. I needed to get you alone and surprised; I needed you to come to the rescue, and then, at the very end of it, I needed you to invite me in the house off hours when your guard was down."

Heidi smirked, sticking out her chest a bit in a prideful posture.

"I see. You kill them. How?"

"Ah, that was easy. It's not my first time, either. That was why I got in trouble back in California. Mostly there, I was playing with hookers. It was fun. But not at all the same thing. Honestly, prostitutes are already half gone anyway. It's in the eyes." Heidi wiggled her fingers in front of her own vision. "Kind of like their soul is vacant. It's really quite sad. Maybe you should do something about that. Well, I guess you won't be able to do much after tonight. I'll write a note for Dr. Mitchell. There's a lot of prostitutes that could use someone like him. He might be able to fix up a couple of them. They'll be more fun to kill that way. But look, it was easy. Drove a truck. I lowered my voice. I wore a baseball cap. I'm pretty sure one of them knew I was a woman. She didn't let on. If anything, I think it put her at ease. It's funny what people are willing to overlook."

Ilse felt a jolt of grief, of anger. "And you just *killed* them? You took them back to the farm?"

"Yes. That was a masterpiece. Look, okay, let me pause. You have to at least give me that. I get the whole fear and anger thing. The confusion and the guilt. But let's pause a moment for you to give me credit for that one." She made a smacking sound with her lips. "A bloody masterpiece. The way you two showed up—that FBI guy. Really impressive. Following those make-believe clues I gave you two. I was truly stunned. I didn't think you'd find it that fast."

"You were down there… You knew we were coming."

"I had to cut myself quick. There was another entrance behind the window. I don't know if you saw that drape. I got there just as you guys came down the stairs. Anyway, I took a little nap on some of my friends that I'd left before. It went exactly as I'd hoped. The sympathy, the waterworks. The, puh-puh-*please*," she said in a fake trembling voice. "Like puppets, all of you. Predictable."

"You killed them to get at me?" Ilse's heart twisted in her chest, and she let out a little sob despite herself, which only prompted a smile on Heidi's face.

"Yes. Well. Also it was fun. But yes, I did kill them to get you. Really it's a bit of both." Heidi tucked her tongue inside her cheek and frowned quizzically. Ilse took that opportunity to slide an inch to the right again, moving even closer to the scissors. Then, with her sister still glancing off, she slid once more.

Heidi seemed lost in her own cleverness, prattling on. "Really, it was all quite easy. Playing with your emotions too, during those sessions, I was so close to laughing more than once. I could see you gazing off as I made up those stories. I could tell that you were thinking about Dad. Thinking about the basement. It was a riot!"

Ilse could feel the fear, but also the guilt. She could feel her face drain, wincing as if in pain. She adjusted, and then used the motion as an excuse to slide even closer to the scissors. "I'm sorry," she murmured.

"Yeah, you're sorry? Like I said, I don't care. You can tell me while you're choking on your own blood."

Ilse kept her calm, kept her tone even, ignoring the comment, trying to stall… just a bit longer. "I don't blame you for hating me. I can't imagine what I did for three weeks after I escaped. I didn't even know Dad was in prison. I didn't know you all had been rescued. I really don't remember any of it. I sometimes wondered if everyone had escaped. Or if I'd imagined it all. It took me years to even remember the basement. And only then, in bits and pieces. And by then, I couldn't even remember where it was except that it was in the Black Forest. I don't know the address. Even now, I don't think I could find it."

"Convenient."

"You're right." Ilse swallowed, closing her eyes and feeling another flicker of guilt and shame. "I hate that I didn't go back for you quick enough. I hate there were others who were suffering. Others I could've helped. I hate it all. I'm so sorry. I know you don't care. But I have to say it."

"Really? Do you mean it?" Heidi's voice softened. She glanced off, biting her lower lip.

"I really mean it."

"Well, if you're *sorry*. I guess… I guess I can forgive you. And then, and then together, we can start over. You and me. Two sisters. You're *sorry*. And I'm sorry. For murdering all those people. They were pleading. Crying. Desperate. I'm sorry for cutting their throats. I stabbed one with an ice pick. I ran over one with a car. I'm so sorry. Sorry. Sorry. Sorry."

Heidi nodded. "Wow. That really works. I feel totally better. Thanks, sis. Hey. Maybe I don't have to kill you after all."

Ilse just watched, grim, scooting once more toward the scissors. Now her elbow brushed the desk. She could feel the cup holder rattle.

"Then again, it does annoy me, just a little bit. You keep trying to grab those scissors. So here's what I'm going to do. I know how much Dad liked using the scissors. Especially on you. That pretty little ear of yours did not get that way by accident. I remember that. You screamed real loud. Such squawking sounds like a crowing rooster. A set of lungs on you. Let me tell you."

Ilse's heart plummeted as Heidi reached past her, grabbing the scissors. She pointed them toward her sister, making a snipping gesture.

"It will be kind of poetic, if you think about it. Yeah. Poetic. That's the word." Heidi grinned. She tapped Ilse on the nose with the cold blades.

"I think I'll kill you with these. But, because you said *sorry*, and frankly, because I believe you meant it," she said, patting Ilse on the head, "I'm going to go ahead and let you decide how I cut you to pieces. All right? One-time offer. And only because I really like you. How would you like me to murder you?"

CHAPTER TWENTY NINE

The fear was complete and the horror at the loss of the scissors settled like silt in Ilse's lungs, making it difficult to even breathe. She was trapped—stuck. No way out. Death seemed imminent. Fear seemed the only emotion remaining, already having flooded through her, already having filled her veins. So much terror…

She blinked, and in her sleep-deprived state she glimpsed two small feet at the top of basement stairs.

She blinked again… The feet were rooted to the concrete. Frozen. Paralyzed.

Ilse inhaled shakily, eyes narrowing now. She wasn't a child anymore. She blinked again, and in her mind's eye, the feet were gone from the top step.

"So that's how it's going to be?" said Ilse, staring wide-eyed at the scissors in her sister's hand.

"That's how it always had to be," sneered Heidi. The scissors flashed down toward Ilse's neck. At the same time, Ilse surged up, *hard.*

Heidi hadn't bound her feet. And while it had been a while since she'd gone to the gym, Ilse had trained for the last five years. Leaving a jujitsu practitioner their feet was always a mistake.

She went for the fifty-fifty position. A style of jujitsu where legs interlocked, allowing further access to one's opponent.

Ilse slid her leg between her sister's, and then twisted. Knees clashed. Legs buckled. Heidi yelled and stumbled, and at the same time, Ilse fell off the couch, using the full force of her weight to bring her sister toppling to the floor. The two of them hit, hard. The scissors went clattering. Ilse wasn't done though. She pushed up, desperately, kicking away and extricating her legs.

She heard Heidi growl, felt fingers scrambling at her leg. Long nails dug into her skin, ripping.

She yelped in pain, but darted forward. Her sister moved to the scissors, lifted them, and swung hard.

Ilse knew what would have to happen next. She knew it would be painful. But it was also the only way to get some distance. She could picture the scissors slamming into her neck. While she was trained in jujitsu, she was only a blue belt. Without her hands, against an armed person, she wouldn't last long at all.

And so she turned, bracing herself, and then flung herself through the window of the patio toward the lake.

Glass shattered. A jagged slice across her cheek. Then shards fell with her, into the backyard. Her shoulder hit the sodden ground. More sharp pain as shards of glass jammed into her shoulder. But Ilse was still moving. She could feel warm blood slipping down her arm. She could feel it slick and wet against her fingertips. Gasping desperately, her fingers scrambling now, moving through the dirt, the fallen leaves, and the old grass, she found shards of glass. Most of them too small. Some of them sharp, jagged, ripping and gouging at her fingertips. She was still fazed from the fall, wincing and shaking her head in the night. Would one of the neighbors have heard the sound? The lake houses were quite far from each other.

Heidi was coming, snarling. She pushed open the patio door and moved down the steps, scissors braced in one hand.

"I'd meant to kill you in a basement," she said, snarling. "I should have guessed you wouldn't have one. For all your psychobabble, you're as scared as you ever were!"

Ilse wasn't in the mood for further taunting, though. She sawed desperately at her ropes with a shard of glass. Blood slipped along her arm, past her elbow, tapping against the grass and the leaves. She winced as more glass cut against her hands and palms. She scrambled in the dirt, kicking back, trying to separate herself from her sister for just a few seconds longer. She could feel the glass shard between her hands, could feel it ripping against the rope binding her wrists.

Her sister jerked forward, slamming down with the scissors.

The rope ripped. Ilse's hands were now free, but both of them were slick with red, both of them in pain.

Scissors flashed across her cheek, but again, Ilse managed to propel Heidi backward with a kick, sending her stumbling into the dust.

Ilse regained her feet, desperately looking for a weapon of her own. There, a discarded branch. She moved toward it, but didn't get far before her sister came hurtling forward, tackling her from the side and sending her ricocheting against a thick trunk.

Ilse wheezed, groaning where her back struck the rigid wood.

She tried to draw breath, to raise her voice and shout for help. The lake houses were really quite far from each other. But surely someone would hear. Before she could yell, though, her sister had lifted the same branch she'd been angling for. Heidi swung it, bringing it bearing down on Ilse's head.

Ilse jolted to the side, but the branch caught her shoulder. She was sent reeling again. Bloodied, bludgeoned, bruised, she fell to one knee.

Heidi screamed. She swung the branch again, aiming for Ilse's head.

But Ilse moved, jerking back. The branch snapped against the trunk of the tree, breaking in half with a geyser of splinters.

The resounding *crack* reverberated in Ilse's ears as she scrambled back. Her sister still held the scissors, but they were low, as she glanced at the broken branch in disgust, and then tossed it off to the side. Instead of retreating further, though, Ilse knew she couldn't keep giving ground. She was bleeding, and her sister was distracted in that moment from the broken branch. And so, instead of continuing backwards, Ilse surged forward instead.

She managed to grab her sister's wrist before Heidi could attack. The two of them hit the ground with yells and snarls.

They rolled closer toward the lake.

Roots and rough ground and a carpet of leaves crunched beneath them as they continued to struggle. The scissors were lost, and Ilse tried to reach for them. Heidi grabbed her fingers, twisting, trying to break them. Ilse managed to yank her hand free. She punched, hard. The martial art she trained didn't teach how to punch, though, and she did little more than bruise her knuckles against the ground.

"Heidi, stop!" Ilse growled. "I don't want to hurt you!"

"*I* want to hurt *you.*"

Heidi reached up, yanking hard at Ilse's hair, pulling at the fringe over her injured ear. At the same time, Ilse broke her sister's grip. They continue to roll, closer to the lake. Ilse shoved off her sister, managing to get a little bit of distance. She took two steps away, but then was tackled from behind and both of them went to the ground again. Something cracked. Ilse felt a sharp jolt of pain, but then realized she'd landed on a dead branch. Hopefully all that had broken was the wood.

She could feel hands scrabbling toward her neck. Could feel thumbs pressing against her throat. Ilse kicked up hard. She caught her sister in the stomach, and propelled her backwards. There was a sudden splash as Heidi tumbled into the shallows of the lake. Murky water swirled around her feet. Heidi growled, rising from the wet, dripping water and soaked to the bone.

The time for talk was over. Both sisters stood for a moment, squared off beneath the moon. Both of them muddy and bloodied. Both of them injured and scraped and bruised. Both of them gasping heavily. Heidi wet, dripping, and Ilse with red hands.

For a moment, Ilse considered stepping back, retreating back to the house. But she was so tired of running away. She faced off with this figment of her past. Was this truly her sister? Perhaps. As good a story as any. Because that's all it was. A story. There was no truth to someone who couldn't remember. It was all just make-believe until the memories lodged back into place. And maybe they never would. Ilse could remember the gasping, the struggling, the shattered glass as she'd been pushed through that small window. She thought she could remember a little cheer rising from her siblings in the basement. She remembered stumbling away, bare feet against pine needles. Then the yelling and the screaming. She had escaped. And she had forgotten. For so long she'd forgotten everything. By the time the memories returned, she thought it was too late to do anything at all. She hadn't even remembered where the house was with that basement until she graduated. And by then, she had taken to cycling through Google maps, looking at the Black Forest. It was far too large for her to guess which house. Had her subconscious known her father was in prison? Her siblings had been loosed? Three weeks too late, apparently. Though all of that was missing. Ilse had long since changed her name. No one had known who she was. No one even suspected she had a history worth hiding. No one except Dr. Mitchell, and he cared about her.

And now a fragment of that past had come like a wraith to haunt her. To kill her. This woman, this poor wretch who claimed to be her sister, had already killed at least seven others. She had intended to kill Ilse too.

Some people went through trauma and recovered, deciding to help. Ilse was not perfect. She had done things she wasn't proud of. She had even hurt others, with her words, and sometimes her actions. She was no saint. But there were others who went through horrors, and then buckled. It almost seemed like something would snap inside of them. Heidi was one such person. She had joined the very monsters who had tormented her as a child..

There was an old phrase. *If you can't beat them, join them.*

And so Heidi had. Like father like daughter.

If you can't beat them, join them.

Ilse certainly wasn't going to join her sister.

She supposed she would just have to beat her then.

CHAPTER THIRTY

Both of them snarled at the same time, and lunged. Fingers went toward throats, and fists flew. Ilse tried to go for the fifty-fifty leg lock again, but this time Heidi saw it coming and retreated back into the shallows. The water swirled into her shoes and socks, soaking. Ilse stumbled in the shallows as well, carried by her own mistaken momentum, sliding on the ground, one leg wet, the other trying to catch her balance. She righted, bringing herself up, but was kicked, a foot colliding with her knee.

Ilse went low in the shallows as well, falling into the water. "Die!" Heidi screamed. She yanked at Ilse's long, dark hair, dragging her head down and bending her over completely. She pulled her sister with feral strength, bodily dragging her into the lake. The two of them splashed in the shallows, rolling and kicking and churning mud. Droplets of wet flecked every which way. The moon watched the two of them struggle, distancing from the shore even further.

Ilse could still stand, barely. She fought, trying to drag herself back to the shore. Both of them were already gasping, heaving. Ilse didn't even want to think what it would feel like to try and breathe underwater.

Heidi's fingers kept yanking at the fistful of hair, pulling Ilse's head toward the liquid, trying to drown her.

Ilse swallowed air just before her head was submerged. Dirty water in her nose, against her sealed lips. Her eyes shut. Her ears resounded with the thrumming echo. She yanked back, shoving hard against her sister. This time, she managed to get her head above water, hair ripped, but even then, Heidi's fingers fell from her slick locks.

Ilse breathed, gulping in air, blinking aside dirty water. She tried to look, but her eyes stung, and blearily, beneath the moon, she only glimpsed a shadow lunging at her again.

Another feral shout. And this time, Ilse felt fingers wrapped tight around her throat. The two of them back underwater again. Heidi on top, Ilse choking, blind in the darkness, submerged beneath the gelid liquid, already desperate for breath, and now with her throat being squeezed.

She felt her shoulder blades hit the silty floor. Her sister had taken her to the very bottom of the shallows in the lake.

No more moon, just oppressive darkness. And mud and dirt and water plants. And a shadow above her, like a ghoul, holding her throat and squeezing and keeping her down.

Panic. Inevitably, panic.

But Ilse reached up, desperately trying to pull at her sister's fingers.

Heidi squeezed even harder, and Ilse could feel black spots forming across her vision. She couldn't breathe. She was already out of air. There, beneath the water, drowning and choking, her sister on top, she didn't feel the pain in her hands or elbow anymore from the glass. She couldn't feel the bruises. All she could feel was the desperate, overwhelming ache in her lungs, as she struggled to swallow air, but choked on silty water instead.

She had often thought drowning might be peaceful. At least at first. But there was nothing peaceful about this experience. Only pain. And throbbing, aching lungs. Desperation and fear.

She managed to rip one of her sister's thumbs off her throat, but Heidi just shoved hard against Ilse's chest.

She wasn't going to let her sister back up. There was no way.

Ilse could feel her consciousness fleeing. She knew she was on the verge of death. Not much longer now.

Bubbles fled past her cheeks, past her lips, and past her nose, swarming toward the surface of the lake. The bubbles fled her, the same way she'd fled that basement. The bubbles fled past her sister, leaving both of them behind, against the base of the lake.

Ilse tried to kick out, but the water softened the blow. And so she fought dirty. There was nothing left. Only one more shot. She was dying.

Both hands up, hard. A dirty move she'd been taught by one of the less reputable sparring partners at the gym. Both fingers gouging up and in. Into her sister's eyes, *hard*.

It wasn't so much of a scream as a burst of bubbles. But she knew she'd scored. Her sister's hands retracted immediately. Ilse could feel the horrible gristle beneath her fingers. But she didn't let go. Fear flooded her. In her mind's eyes she glimpsed two mismatched eyes. One blue, one brown, staring at her.

She yelled incoherently beneath the water, but there was no more air to give. No sound followed. Again, she was voiceless, trapped in the dark, alone. Fighting for her life.

Two mismatched eyes. And so she squeezed, hard. Not letting go. Her thumbs jammed into her sister's eyes, and she could feel something give. A horrible, terrible sensation.

She felt Heidi shudder and flail, desperately trying to shove Ilse off.

Only then, once she was sure she'd caused damage, did Ilse let go. She kicked twice, pushing off the silty floor and rising to the surface of the lake. Her head burst out to meet the moon, her lungs wheezed, and water splashed around her as she desperately inhaled.

She choked on strands of liquid at the same time as drawing breath. She bent over, gagging and hacking and coughing, but still managing to breathe in between.

Her sister was stumbling around, holding her face and groaning. Blood fled past her fingers, staining her knuckles and trickling to her hands before dripping back into the lake. Droplets of crimson marred the otherwise gray liquid beneath the moon.

Heidi gasped even further and stood up in the shallows, drenched and soaked and exhausted and broken. The wet seemed to quench some fire in Ilse, and she shivered, feeling so very cold all of a sudden… She should have run. This was all a mistake. What was she even doing? Her own sister, bloodied, blinded.

Because of Ilse.

She'd promised, her entire life, to help those tormented by people like her father. To help people like her sister… But now… now it was all too horrible. She felt a sudden urge to vomit.

"Stop!" Ilse said, pleading, her voice choked with a sob.

Her sister looked over. One eye horribly punctured, blind. The other one squinting so badly, there was almost no way she could see.

But Heidi was determined. She howled and came charging.

"Stop!" Ilse screamed. "Please. I don't want to hurt—"

Too late. Her sister met her, hard. A knee caught her stomach. Fingers went toward Ilse's eyes now. But she stumbled back.

Splashing, desperate, slipping on the mud and twigs and leaves, but reaching the shore, while reeling backwards, away. Heidi kept coming, charging, splashing as well, sending sprays of droplets every which way.

Ilse reached the shore first. She saw the scissors. Grabbed them.

Her sister couldn't see much of anything. Blood poured from her eyes, spreading out like a root system beneath the trees.

"Stop!" Ilse yelled, desperately.

Her sister just kept coming. Heidi blinked, gasping, only shifting last moment as if catching something out of the corner of her eye. She angled toward Ilse again, hands extended, surging forward.

Ilse held the scissors, pointing them at her sister. “Don’t—”

Heidi charged. She’d killed seven already. She wanted to kill another.

Ilse didn’t know what to do. She didn’t know—

They both went down hard. A root struck the back of Ilse’s head. Stars danced across her vision. She groaned, aching, bloodied and exhausted.

For a moment, she half expected her sister’s hands to be around her throat again.

Except they weren’t.

It took her a moment to recover her senses, struggling against the blow. But as her eyes fluttered, as she tried to sit up, slowly, gradually, she realized her sister had gone limp.

Struggling, Ilse extricated her legs, rolling her sister off her where she sat amidst the roots of the tree.

Heidi fell limply, one arm hitting the ground with a dull *thump*.

The purple-handled scissors were buried in her sister’s neck.

Heidi give a shuddering little gasp, her throat emitting an odd, off-putting wheezing sound. She tried to choke out a word, but then broke into a fit of coughing, her hands limp at her side, her eyes fluttering.

“Heidi!” Ilse said, her voice shrill. “Hang on. Just hold on!”

Her sister’s eyes fluttered again, then closed. Ilse yelled in despair, hurrying over. But as she neared, her sister’s eyes snapped open again. Heidi smiled, blood showing along her teeth, her eyes like pale and broken moons in the dark.

Ilse breathed heavily, desperately. Then, with trembling fingers, in agony and pain, she pushed off the leaf-strewn ground. She pulled the scissors from Heidi’s neck and placed her hand around her sister’s throat.

“Hang on,” she said, desperately. “I told you not to. I told you.” She finally managed to draw breath long enough to scream. “Help!” she yelled. “Please, someone, help!”

“Father wasn’t alone,” Heidi said, gasping and choking out the words. “Not…” She tried to swallow, but then just winced and wheezed instead. Her words were weak as if it took every last ounce of breath to simply utter them. “Not alone upstairs.”

Ilse blinked, stunned, but kept her hands held to her sister’s throat, holding back the blood as best she could. Her own blood fell from her fingers, from the cuts on her arms and elbow and shoulder. From the gouge marks in her face. Their blood mingled, intermixed. It fell to the ground, amidst the dirt, creating mud.

"Help, please, someone!" She looked back at her sister, whose devastated eyes had rolled back. She lowered her voice for the faintest moment, whispering. "What do you mean he wasn't alone?"

Heidi was still now, though. Her chest no longer rising and falling, her eyes sealed. She let out a final little croaking breath, letting loose a sound like a puff of vapor to the sky. With it, hidden in the strangled sound of gasping pain, Ilse thought she heard a word… A single, resonant word. "…upstairs…"

And then Heidi went entirely still.

Ilse forgot to breathe for a moment, staring wide-eyed at her sister's still form. "What do you mean?" she said, desperately. "What do you mean?" she screamed. "He had an accomplice? Heidi? Heidi, wake up! What do you mean?" But her sister didn't answer, and Ilse cursed, raising her voice and shouting even louder. "Please! Someone help! We need help!"

She heard barking from the neighbor's house. She glimpsed orange lights suddenly flare on the porch.

"Help!" she screamed, even louder. "Call the police. Call an ambulance!"

Her sister wasn't moving. She wasn't breathing. She wasn't even twitching. But Ilse held on for dear life. Still yelling at the top of her lungs. Still desperately trying to call for help.

Help was in such short supply these days.

She'd tried to help. Tried to help a woman she'd known as Samantha.

And the same woman had to tried to kill her.

Her fingers were slick. Her hands trembling from the cold and exhaustion. And yet she still held her hand against the neck of the woman who had tried to kill her. Hoping beyond hope she could save her life.

No breathing though; no movement. Any ambulance was already too far away.

Sometimes, no matter how much someone tried, they simply couldn't help.

CHAPTER THIRTY ONE

Ilse winced as the paramedics probed at her arm, wrapping her elbow in another layer of bandages. Soon, she felt she'd end up like some mummy with the amount of gauze they seemed intent on using.

Still, she didn't protest, preferring to sit on the porch steps facing the street. An ambulance and six police cars lined the road. She watched as an unmarked sedan pulled up behind the ambulance. A thin man with a baseball cap and a flannel shirt exited the car, moving around the ambulance and angling toward Ilse's driveway.

She watched as Agent Tom Sawyer approached her house, glancing toward the lake, the trees, then up at the two paramedics and their patient on the patio steps.

Sawyer moved toward Ilse just as a couple of coroner's assistants emerged from behind the house, carrying a stretcher with a sheet over a still lump.

Ilse stared at the lump and shivered, looking away and off toward the leaves scattering the road.

Sawyer watched the coroner's assistants pass by before joining Ilse on the steps. The paramedics made room as the FBI agent sat next to Ilse, staring out at the leaf-strewn road as well.

Ilse smelled the faint odor of alcohol as a wipe was run over her fingers for what felt like the millionth time. "I'm fine," she muttered, gently pushing away the hands of the nearest paramedic. "Really. It's worse than it looks."

Her clothes were still damp, her hair plastered against the side of her face. It made it difficult to hide her maimed ear, but for the moment, she didn't really care. She heard the sound of the coroner's assistants trying to navigate the driveway with the body, but she refused to look over.

A couple of police were now rounding the house, small plastic evidence bags gripped in their hands, their latex gloves visible past their lowered sleeves as they scanned the glass enclosure of the patio seating. It would cost a fortune to get that shattered window replaced, she was nearly sure of it.

Ilse closed her eyes briefly, inhaling through her nose. Agent

Sawyer remained sitting next to her, his hands clasped in front of his knees. He didn't smell of cologne or aftershave, or anything really, save the faintest odor of wood shavings… or maybe sawdust.

She glanced at him, then at his flannel shirt. "You a lumberjack in your spare time?"

"Hmm?"

"You smell like wood chips."

"Oh. No. I whittle."

"Whittle. Of course you do."

She nodded slowly, wincing at the motion and steadying her head. Even her wrists ached from where they'd been rubbed raw. Her fingers were also covered in bandages from where glass had gouged. The paramedics had managed to remove the shards, thankfully.

The two medics gave her another once-over, but at a look from Sawyer, they retreated back in the direction of the ambulance, watching warily from behind the parked vehicle.

Ilse found she could breathe a bit easier as they left, leaving her and Agent Sawyer sitting on the front steps, facing the road. Behind her, she could hear officers moving through the house, and others combing the back yard toward the lake.

"So," Sawyer said, quietly. "What happened?"

"I already gave my statement to the cop. Some detective guy."

"Lopez?"

"Yeah; I think so. He didn't seem to like *you* very much. When I asked where you were, he looked like he'd swallowed a lemon."

"You okay?"

Ilse's fingers trembled for a moment where she rested them daintily across one of her legs. Perhaps it was the painkillers, or the pain itself, but her eyes went misty for a brief moment. She swallowed, clearing her throat, and said, "I don't know."

Sawyer didn't say anything, but remained sitting next to her, watching the road.

"She was the actual killer," Ilse said, softly. "Heidi. My client. The woman I thought we rescued. She was the one who killed them. All of them. When I brought her home… she was looking at the doors, at the locks and windows. I thought she was scared… Now, I think she was just checking the entry and exit points. She stole my pepper spray from my keychain. She wanted to kill me."

"Why?"

Ilse paused now. Of course, she couldn't tell him everything. She couldn't even tell him most things. Certainly not about Heidi claiming she was Ilse's sister, and how Ilse couldn't even remember her. Not about the basement back in the Black Forest. Not about the repressed memories, or the two mismatched eyes.

Not about any of it.

So she sighed and simply said, "Psychotic break. From her own trauma. Really sad when you think about it." She trailed off, shivering.

A hand descended lightly on her shoulder, and for a moment, she jolted, surprised. Sawyer didn't lower his hand at first, but instead just looked at her, his green, stubborn gaze softening somewhat. "Sorry," he murmured, quietly. "Sorry you went through that."

She stared at him for a moment, stunned. His hand felt very warm against her shoulder and she felt a jolt of regret when he removed it, folding it in his lap and turning to face the road again, a quiet sadness in his own posture.

For a moment, sitting there, his shirt brushing against her shoulder, she wanted to say more. Maybe it was his way with few words, or simply his silent presence. Maybe it was just her desperate need to *tell* someone. But a part of her wanted to say more. To confide in Agent Sawyer. To tell him…

Something.

But then she swallowed, and the desire vanished just as quickly. Who was she kidding anyway? If she told anyone… told an FBI agent of all people, she'd probably be locked up herself. No one would believe her. And even if they did, she wouldn't even know where to start. She barely remembered.

No. Some things were best left unsaid.

"Do me," said Sawyer suddenly.

She stared at him. "Excuse you?"

"You know what I mean. You're a shrink, right?" He glanced at her bandages, and gave a little nod of approval. "Not bad for a couch-sitter."

"Couch-sitter? Is that what you think therapists do?"

"It isn't?"

"Do you in what way?"

"Read me. Like you do. Back at the station, you seemed to think I'd gotten in trouble with my boss."

"So you did?" Ilse said, surprised at this volunteered piece of information.

Sawyer just shrugged. "Do me."

"You want me to diagnose you?"

He scratched at his chin, then gave a bobbing nod.

Ilse watched him for a moment, her own eyes narrowed in thought. She wasn't sure how much she wanted to say. She'd botched it all so badly with Heidi—she couldn't have been more wrong. Then again, at the same time, she knew she was good at her job. One of the best, in fact.

She wasn't sure why, but a part of her wanted to impress the quiet, understated BAU agent. So she rattled off in quick succession, "I can't give a diagnosis. Not without some time. But I did pick up some things… You're recently divorced. A loner. I'd guess you don't have many, if any, friends. Your family probably checks in on you now and then, but mostly by phone. You're the sort that might use a term like 'married to the job' unironically. You value loyalty above all else. You're honest, and hate liars."

"Hmm. Nah."

"Nah?" Ilse said. "Most of that is definitely accurate. I'd stake my job on it."

"No family."

"Oh. Well… How about the rest of it?"

Sawyer gave her a long look, and then got to his feet slowly, dusting off his jeans and clearing his throat. "You did good out there," he said. " Agency could use someone like you, you know."

Ilse stared at him. "What?"

"I don't really care about that therapy stuff. But you killed a serial murderer with a pair of craft scissors." He shrugged. "Impressive."

And then he turned, whistling softly as he moved around the side of the house, toward where Ilse had last seen Detective Lopez.

As he left, she glanced back beneath her mailbox and spotted the corner of a piece of paper beneath a pile of freshly fallen leaves. She frowned, reaching out and plucking out the second postcard.

She turned it over. *Hilda Mueller.*

She sighed softly. That chapter was now behind her. Lucky—that's what she was. Very, lucky. She could have ended up like her sister, messed up from the very beginning. Barely a chance to speak of. It was all so horrible and sad. Ilse sighed. At least she knew the source of the postcards. She carefully tore the thing in half. Then again, and again, until there was nothing but tiny pieces of confetti between her fingers.

She winced where her fingers pressed too hard against the paper, but then held a small pile of the tattered fragments cupped in one hand.

She waited for a moment for the sound of the breeze to rise, the wind to sweep through, the trees to rustle.

And then she tossed the handful of paper pieces into the air, watching as the wind caught them and sent them fluttering away, over the rail, and across the ground until the postcard was nothing more than a bad memory.

***

A weekend of mostly sleeping and rescheduling appointments allowed Ilse some level of refreshment. But Monday morning still came quicker than she would have liked. She'd refreshed the bandages on her fingers, though the gauze around her elbow she'd left the same. She stooped over a small bowl of homemade oatmeal next to the wood-burning stove, inhaling the odor of cinnamon and crushed pistachios.

She was now wearing a green turtleneck and another pair of unmarked sweatpants. She glanced at the old analog clock over the stove.

8:54.

Six minutes and she could get up and unlock the front door for the first client of the day. This time, an old client she'd been seeing for more than a year.

She wouldn't swear off new clients. Not at all. But for the next few days, Ilse had decided it would be nice to meet with people she knew.

8:55. Only five minutes left. She smiled in anticipation, but remained seated. One had to be precise in things such as these.

As she took another spoonful of milky granola, her phone began to buzz. Frowning, Ilse fished out the old flip phone, raising it. "Dr. Beck's office," she said automatically.

"Doc?" said a voice on the other end.

"Agent Sawyer?"

"Mhmm. Hey, I spoke with the office here."

"Oh? About what?"

Agent Sawyer cleared his throat uncomfortably, and a long pause stretched. Then, quickly, he said, "You did good work. Look, what do you think about being a consultant for the field office? When murder cases come up."

Ilse blinked in surprise, stunned. "I—are you serious?"

"You were right about one thing yesterday. I do value loyalty. But also competence. You displayed both. Well? Interested?"

Ilse shivered, closing her eyes against the memories of yesterday. But then she opened them again, allowing the recollections to play across her subconscious. Instead of cringing back from the pain of the thoughts, she allowed them to sweep past her, running their course, but leaving her undisturbed. A moment later, after the guilt, the sadness, the grief had slipped away again, she said, hesitantly, "Are you sure? I thought you didn't put much stock in us therapists."

"You caught a killer I missed. Besides, a guy could use some allies around these parts."

For a moment, she wondered if he'd meant to use the word "friends." Then again, that was probably just the therapist in her jumping to conclusions. For a second, it was her turn to drift off into contemplative silence, leaving Sawyer waiting for her response on the other end.

At last, she cleared her throat and said, simply, "All right. I'd like to help."

She wasn't even sure why she'd said it at first. The memories of the previous day came swishing past a second time. She'd failed her sister—hadn't even remembered her. She hadn't gone back. Hadn't even remembered the old house until years later. She'd let her father, her tormentor, exact whatever he wanted on the rest of them. She'd left them helpless.

Sometimes, as a therapist, she had the opportunity to help the survivors of serial killers and violent criminals.

But what if she had a chance to intervene before the damage was done? Was this a type of absolution? Was she responding out of sentiment? Whatever the case, she'd given her answer.

"Good," said Sawyer, simply. He cleared his throat as if wanting to add something else, but then decided against it. The phone went silent.

Ilse glanced down, double-checking that the FBI agent had hung up. Then she sighed, massaging the bridge of her nose and lowering the device.

When she looked up again, with a start, she realized the clock now read 8:59.

Only a minute left to be precise. She cursed, jolting from her seat, wincing against the pain in her arm.

She hurried to the front door, glancing at the second clock over the patio entryway. She paused by the door, one hand on the handle, gripping it, but waiting. She watched the second hand tick by. Five… four…three…

She was glad she'd said yes to Agent Sawyer. Yes. Glad. That was the right word.

But absolution wouldn't end there. She had unfinished business. Her sister had mentioned something as she'd died. Mentioned her father had an accomplice upstairs…

Ilse needed to find that house. She needed to find that accomplice.

And she needed to find her father.

Ilse was no longer a child. No longer glued to the top of those basement steps. No longer willing to live in fear. *Take captive every thought*... It was all long overdue. Time was ticking. He visited her so often in her memories; well, now it was her turn to go to *him.*

NOW AVAILABLE!

NOT LIKE HE SEEMED
(An Ilse Beck FBI Suspense Thriller—Book 2)

NOT LIKE HE SEEMED (An Ilse Beck FBI Suspense Thriller) is book #2 in a new series by mystery and suspense author Ava Strong.

FBI Special Agent Ilse Beck, victim of a traumatic childhood in Germany, moved to the U.S. to become a renowned psychologist specializing in PTSD, and the world's leading expert in the unique trauma of serial-killer survivors. By studying the psychology of their survivors, Ilse has a unique and unparalleled expertise in the true psychology of serial killers. She had no idea, though, that she would become an FBI agent herself.

The FBI desperately needs Ilse's help in catching the "Alphabet Killer"—an unhinged serial killer who seems to be arranging his victims' bodies into the shapes of letters. Is he spelling a word? Hinting at who will be his next victim?

Or is he far more cunning and deranged than anyone could imagine?

Ilse, meanwhile, plagued by her own past, realizes the time has come to face her demons and revisit the site of her childhood home in Germany. But will the trip help her expunge her own dark memories—or push her over the edge?

A dark and suspenseful crime thriller, the ILSE BECK series is a breathtaking page-turner, unputdownable from the first word. A compelling and perplexing mystery, rife with twists and jaw-dropping secrets, it will make you fall in love with a brilliant new character, while it keeps you shocked late into the night.

Books #3 and #4 in the series—NOT LIKE YESTERDAY and NOT LIKE THIS—are also available.

Ava Strong

Debut author Ava Strong is author of the REMI LAURENT mystery series, comprising three books (and counting); of the ILSE BECK mystery series, comprising four books (and counting); and of the STELLA FALL psychological suspense thriller series, comprising three books (and counting).

An avid reader and lifelong fan of the mystery and thriller genres, Ava loves to hear from you, so please feel free to visit http://www.avastrongauthor.com to learn more and stay in touch.

BOOKS BY AVA STRONG

REMI LAURENT FBI SUSPENSE THRILLER
THE DEATH CODE (Book #1)
THE MURDER CODE (Book #2)
THE MALICE CODE (Book #3)

ILSE BECK FBI SUSPENSE THRILLER
NOT LIKE US (Book #1)
NOT LIKE HE SEEMED (Book #2)
NOT LIKE YESTERDAY (Book #3)
NOT LIKE THIS (Book #4)

STELLA FALL PSYCHOLOGICAL SUSPENSE THRILLER
HIS OTHER WIFE (Book #1)
HIS OTHER LIE (Book #2)
HIS OTHER SECRET (Book #3)

www.ingramcontent.com/pod-product-compliance
Lightning Source LLC
Chambersburg PA
CBHW020322030826
48979CB00022B/731

* 9 7 8 1 0 9 4 3 9 2 1 4 1 *